JUSTIFIED BURDEN

BROTHERHOOD PROTECTORS WORLD

LORI MATTHEWS

Twisted Page Press LLC

BROTHERHOOD PROTECTORS

ORIGINAL SERIES BY ELLE JAMES

For Kelly Eager.

Our days by the pool will be back again soon.

ACKNOWLEDGMENTS

As always my heartfelt thanks goes out to a great many people who helped make this book possible. My deepest gratitude my editors, Corinne DeMaagd and Heidi Senesac for their patience and guidance; my cover artist, Lyndsey Llewellen, Llewellen Designs for making my story come alive: my virtual assistant who is a social media guru and all round dynamo, Susan Poirier. My friends who talk me off the ledge this year more than most: Janna MacGregor, Suzanne Burke, Stacey Wilk and Kimberley Ash. My mother and my sisters whose support I value so highly. My husband and my children who not only support me but add to my stories in innumerable ways. Thanks for all of your great ideas! You all are my world. And a special heartfelt thanks goes out to you, the reader. The fact you are reading this means my dreams have come true.

A special thanks to Elle James for trusting me with her characters and her world. I am profoundly grateful.

JUSTIFIED BURDEN

Former Navy SEAL, and Personal Security Specialist Rhys Bennett is in Canyon Springs to mend after being shot on his last assignment. His wound has healed and it's almost time for him to go back to work, but he's worried. The sixth sense that's kept him alive so far is MIA.

For Scarlett Jones, being in Canyon Springs is her chance at a fresh start after a devastating tragedy. She's desperate for her design business to be successful. But when things keep going wrong on her latest remodel, panic sets in. Is someone sabotaging the worksite on purpose or is it all in her head?

Realizing the distracting Scarlett is in trouble, Rhys puts aside his self-doubt and volunteers to protect her. Watching over the beautiful redhead won't be too difficult. Or so he thinks until a body is discovered and the mystery surrounding Scarlett turns potentially deadly. Will Rhys be up to the task of keeping Scarlett safe or will the killer get away with murder twice?

CHAPTER 1

SCARLETT JONES'S heart swelled as she pulled into the parking lot of the Wellness Retreat at Canyon Springs. She was proud of the redesign she'd done, and when it opened in two and a half short weeks, everyone would finally see it.

After parking, she climbed out of her SUV. It was still dark and somewhere near the twenty-degree mark. She shivered. So many Christmas songs talked up snow, and having a white Christmas had sounded so jolly when she lived in California. The reality was less cheerful and more bone-chilling, especially at five a.m.. Being awake at this hour was a crime against nature, she was sure. At least against her nature.

The freezing air stung her cheeks and chin as she hurried around the back of the SUV to open the hatch. Why did she choose to live somewhere that her face hurt from the cold? She tried humming "Jingle Bells" to brighten her mood as she gathered all her bags and her notebooks in her arms, but it didn't help. When Scarlett stepped back to close the tailgate by swinging her foot under the sensor, she slipped on the icy snow and almost ended up on her butt. Regaining her balance, Scarlett tried again. The tailgate closed this time, and she slowly picked her way across the parking lot toward the building.

She glanced down at her boots. They were a beautiful forest green leather that matched her coat exactly. And her eyes. She had bought them on a whim, not knowing how friggin' cold it was in Canyon Springs in winter. Her toes were frozen, and she hadn't made it more than ten feet. It didn't help the boots had spike heels. Scarlett sighed. They had seemed like such a good idea in L.A.

She stepped up onto the cleared sidewalk and breathed a sigh of relief. She moved quickly toward the building's entryway. After shuffling the items in her arms, she started to rummage through her purse for the set of keys her boss, Sunny Travers, had given her. She stopped a few feet from the main doors as she dug deeper in her purse. She heard a sound and looked up to see a masked person barreling from the building, straight toward her.

She started to scream, but the intruder tackled her like a linebacker. Scarlett went airborne and flew backward, landing hard on her behind. The masked intruder took off at a run while Scarlett was still sitting on the ground, trying to inflate her lungs.

Finally, able to suck in oxygen, Scarlett let out the yell that had been building in her throat. What the fuck just happened? She let go of everything in her arms and took a few breaths. Then she checked herself for injuries. All her limbs still seemed to work, although she wasn't sure about her toes. They were numb. She moved gingerly, getting onto her knees. Her butt was killing her. Could you break your ass? She tried not to rub her backside as she slowly climbed to her feet.

She needed to call the police. A flash of her mother and a room full of cops milling around filled her mind's eye. A tremor overtook her whole body. No. She shook her head. She wasn't going there. *Focus.*

She thought about calling the cops again. But what would she tell them? *Someone wearing a balaclava barreled into me and sent me flying backward where I landed on my butt.* She didn't even know if it was a man or a woman. The jacket had been too puffy to describe the person's build and they were about average height. Absolutely none of that was helpful.

She hadn't even seen the person break in. Maybe it was just some rude jerk who had a right to be there, or it was possible they hadn't seen her. Yeah, right. It had been the perfect hockey check. The only thing missing was the skates. Still, it didn't look like anything was amiss. If she called the cops, they would ask her all kinds of questions. She bit her lip. Maybe she should go in and assess the situation first.

Scarlett gathered her things. Moving carefully, she then turned and grabbed the door with one gloved hand. Taking a deep breath, she pulled the door open. She stuck her head in and took a peek around. Seeing nothing alarming, she took a small step inside, making as little noise as possible.

The foyer of the Wellness Retreat building looked just as it had when she'd left the previous evening. It was dark with only one light still burning, but Scarlett couldn't see any sign that anything was amiss. Not that she'd be able to tell anyway. The lobby was still under construction.

There was a temporary work desk set up in the front, but other than that, it was just a large open space with unpainted sheetrock walls. The bright orange X spray-painted on the concrete floor that marked where the reception desk would be was still there, and the base of the fountain that would be part of an impressive display on one wall was intact behind it.

Scarlett dumped her stuff on the temporary desk knocking off the stuffed moose. If the moose was on the desk then Andy and his painting crew definitely weren't here yet. It was their signal. She picked up the moose and put it back on the desk and then moved cautiously down the hallway that led to the medical wing. It, too, looked perfectly fine. Well, fine was an exaggeration. Still a work in progress, ladders, tarps, brooms, and bits of debris were everywhere. Tool chests were tucked out of the way in the corners, but nothing seemed odd or out of place.

Scarlett took a quick look through most of the rooms, but nothing popped out at her. What had the intruder been doing here? Stealing tools? She'd heard that was a frequent problem at construction sites, yet she didn't recall seeing anything in the person's hands. Maybe she'd arrived before they could pull off whatever they'd been planning.

A wave of relief washed over her. If nothing had been tampered with, she wouldn't have to call the cops but she should probably tell Sunny. She sighed. She wasn't looking forward to having that conversation either. Maybe she'd think on it a bit longer. She had too much to do today to waste any more time on the mysterious masked person.

She walked back toward the front and opened the door to the medical wing waiting area.

"Oh. My. God." Scarlett blinked in disbelief. "Holy shit!"

This couldn't be happening. This wasn't real. It couldn't be. Her knees wobbled as she tried to move. She put her hand on the wall for support and then instantly jerked it back as if burned. She looked down at her palm. It was red. Bright red. Scarlett, in fact. The whole room was. Scarlett's belly rolled, and she swallowed hard. She was not going to get sick. She blinked hard. Crying was not an option either.

The workers had painted the waiting area a soft gray yesterday, a lovely contrast to the darker gray carpet. She'd seen the finished product last night. Sunny was coming by to see it today, and Scarlett hoped she would be pleased with everything. This was Scarlett's first big project in Canyon Springs. It had to be perfect.

Now bright red paint dripped down each wall and onto the new rug. There were two empty red paint cans on their sides in the middle of the room. Guess she knew what the masked intruder had been doing, but why? And now what the hell was she going to do?

CHAPTER 2

RHYS BECKETT STUCK GLOVED hands in his jacket pockets, not that it would make a bit of difference. It was so cold he expected polar bears to come wandering by any second. He stomped his feet on the snow-packed ground to get some feeling back into his toes. His boots were usually warm enough, but this cold snap was killing him.

He twisted his arm, keeping his hand in his pocket and glanced at his watch once more. Where was Hudson? He didn't want to text because it would mean taking his winter gloves off. Rhys couldn't text with these gloves on. Hell, he couldn't text without gloves. Phones weren't made for men with big fingers.

Rhys paced in front of the outbuilding that someone had converted into a cabin with a full front porch. The trees that lined the cabin on both sides were laden with the recent snow. Rhys walked over to the fence on the edge of the steep hill. It was a long way down, but the view of the snow-covered ranch and the valley below was incredible, especially as the sun lowered in the sky. It looked like a Christmas card.

A pang of guilt rose in his chest. He should be going home to see his sisters in North Carolina. They always got together at Christmas. But he hadn't told them about the gunshot wound to his leg, and if they found out now, he'd never have any peace.

He rubbed his wound. The doctor had told him he was as good as new, but Rhys had his doubts. Maybe physically he was okay, but he couldn't forget how quickly it had all happened. He'd lost focus just for an instant, and that's all it took. He wasn't sure he still had it in him to be a personal security specialist. Being in charge of someone's safety was a heavy burden. What if he'd lost his edge permanently? He couldn't shake that fear.

He stomped his feet again and swore. Whatever health benefit he'd convinced himself he'd get by walking here from the main house had ceased to seem important ten minutes after he started. Now, forty minutes later, he was quite sure he was going to freeze to death. He was just glad Huck hadn't come with him.

Rhys smiled to himself. Truth was, Huck had abandoned *him*. Smart dog. He'd followed Rhys to the door willingly enough, but the moment Rhys opened it, letting in a waft of winter air, Huck immediately shot him an aggrieved look and then padded back over to his comfy bed next to the heater.

"I should've listened to you, Huck," Rhys mumbled.

Just then, he heard the rumbling of an engine coming up the driveway behind the cabin. He moved toward the sound. The engine cut out and a door opened.

"About damn time!" he growled. "It's so F-ing cold I'm about to lose my right nut to frostbite! What took you so long?" he demanded as he rounded the far corner of the cabin.

"Um..." A tall redhead dressed in a green coat with matching boots stood next to a SUV, one eyebrow raised and her arms full of bags.

Rhys stopped dead and blinked. *What in the hell?* "Ah, I was expecting someone else."

The redhead smiled. "Clearly. Hudson said to tell you he's sorry he couldn't be here. He got held up on a job."

"Great," Rhys said through clenched teeth.

"So, why the right nut?"

"Excuse me?" Rhys stared at the stranger.

She smiled. "You said you were going to lose your right nut to frostbite. Why the right and not the left? Is there something special about it?"

Rhys blinked. Who the hell was this woman, and

why was she talking about his right nut? Her lips curved upward into a big smile that hit him like a rubber bullet to the chest. His lungs froze. This woman was gorgeous. Her eyes sparkled with laughter and made his insides warm up like he'd just downed a bourbon shot.

"The right one hangs out more. The left just likes to stay closer to home," he said with a smile.

"Well, as long as there's a reason." She grinned and shifted the stuff in her arms.

"Oh, sorry." Rhys strode over to her and put his hands out as an offer to help.

She smiled and handed him several bags. "Thanks. You must be Rhys. Hudson described you perfectly." She moved toward a set of small steps that led to the back door.

"Oh, did he? And what did he say?" Rhys asked as he attempted to check out the redhead's ass. The coat was covering it, but he admired her long legs in those crazy boots. Who wore spike heels in the snow like this?

She laughed and glanced over her shoulder at him. "He said you would be the tall, cranky one standing around freezing your nuts off." She dug in her purse and produced a set of keys then shook them triumphantly. "I'd say he got it exactly right."

Rhys pasted a smile on his face while he planned Hudson's slow, agonizing death. Leave it to Hudson to not mention the woman at all. He watched her unlock the door. She looked familiar to him some-how. Like he should know her from somewhere. Except he was pretty sure he would have remem-bered her if they'd met.

"I'm Scarlett, by the way, Scarlett Jones." She unlocked the door and pushed it open.

"The decorator," Rhys said. Maybe that's why he knew her. Hudson had actually mentioned her a couple of times, but Rhys hadn't paid much attention. He'd sure as hell be paying attention now.

"I'm an interior designer," she corrected him quickly.

Rhys stepped inside the cabin. "Um, sorry. Designer. You're the one who redid the ranch for Hudson's mom, and you're redoing the spa now, right?"

Scarlett nodded. "Wellness Retreat. Yes, that's right."

Something was up at the spa. He could tell from the way her forehead wrinkled when she said its name--but he wasn't gonna ask. Not his business.

Scarlett pushed open the door and said, "Ta-da!"

Rhys blinked. Had she expected balloons to tumble from the ceiling when she opened the door? He glanced into the cabin but didn't see anything out of the ordinary, other than it was quite a bit nicer than he'd expected. The main room was dominated by the stone fireplace to his right, which went all the way to the ceiling, and there was a picture window across the room that allowed him to see the amazing view of the valley.

Scarlett looked at him expectantly. He was obviously missing something, but he honestly had no clue what was going on. "Ah, so, why am I here?"

"Sorry?" Scarlett asked. The pinch was back in the middle of her forehead.

"Hudson just told me to meet him here, but he never said why." Rhys glanced through the doorway at the cabin again.

"Oh, well"—she bit her lip—"I guess he wanted me to tell you." She shrugged and gestured for him to enter the cabin.

"After you." Rhys nodded to her and then took off his Stetson. He was new to cowboy hats. He hated that they didn't fully cover his ears, but he liked that they kept the snow off his head. Maybe he'd use earmuffs under it next time.

Scarlett walked in. She stopped in the middle of the room and then turned toward him with her arms splayed open like a game show host. "This is for you."

Rhys struggled to keep from grinning. For just a second, he'd thought she meant *she* was for him. Life was just not that kind.

Scarlett paused. Her smile faltered. Then a flush crawled up her neck to her cheeks until they matched the color of her hair. Rhys laughed out loud.

"Don't be getting any ideas, cowboy. I meant the

cabin. The cabin is for you," Scarlett said, her eyes narrowing as she spoke.

Rhys nodded but still didn't stop grinning. She looked so cute when she blushed. He was having more fun than he'd had in months. More fun than he'd had since he was shot, that was for damn sure.

Scarlett turned away from him and walked over to look out the front window.

Rhys decided to let her off the hook. "So, the cabin's for me to do what with?" he asked.

She turned back around, her coloring back to normal. "What do you mean?"

"What does Hudson want me to do with it? Does it need some work done, or does he need it secured?"

She shook her head. "No. No. Hudson had me redo it. For you. So you can live here. He thought you might be tired of living with him at the ranch house since Sunny is with him most of the time. He said he feels bad that you keep leaving the room to give them space. He wanted you to have a place to relax that was all yours."

Rhys froze. He couldn't breathe. His? "What?" he managed to croak out. He struggled to make sense of the words she was saying. It was too overwhelming. The idea of having his own place in Canyon Springs wasn't something he'd even considered.

Scarlett smiled. "He thinks very highly of you. He asked me to make sure it was...how did he put it? 'Comfortable in a manly way but not too macho.' He said you didn't have patience for men who tried to be macho. I hope you like what I've done."

Rhys looked around the cabin and tried to take it all in. The weight of her gaze on him was distracting. He wasn't used to being in the spotlight. Words failed him.

"You...don't like it?" Her voice was soft. Her shoulders drooped, and her smile disappeared. "I can change any part of it or all of it. Please just let me know what you'd like to see, and I'll make it happen." She took the bags he was holding, brought them over to the sofa, and placed them on the cushions. "I have books in here we can look at. I also have my design boards for the cabin out in my SUV. I can grab them, and we can discuss what you would prefer." She started moving toward the door.

Rhys grabbed her arm when she was parallel to him. "I—"

"It's okay. If you don't like it, we'll change it so it makes you happy. Everyone's home should be their happy place."

"No. You don't understand." He looked into her beautiful green eyes. "I love it. I'm just floored. I didn't expect anything like this. It's a bit..."

"Overwhelming?" Scarlett asked.

Rhys smiled at her. "Yes, overwhelming. That's a good word for it." He took a moment to soak in the cabin.

The couch facing the fireplace was upholstered

with a rich brown leather, the kind of thing he would have chosen for himself, although there were red throw pillows on it, which he wouldn't have bothered with but had to admit they looked nice. A plaid blanket was slung over the back, and a large flat screen TV hung on the wall just above the mantel. The coffee table and the rug beneath it were simple but nice, and a chair facing the window matched the look of the couch.

The kitchen area, to his left, boasted stainless-steel appliances and an island. The small dining area was across from it, in front of another big window, and the table and chairs matched the look of the rest of the pieces.

Scarlett had decorated the whole room in browns and blues with splashes of color, but the best part was the Christmas tree off to his right. It was huge and reached the ceiling. Lights and multicolored ornaments decorated the branches. He'd never had a tree of his own. Somewhere inside him, a little boy was jumping up and down over having his own tree. With so many sisters, he'd never been able to have a say on anything to do with Christmas. Now he could do what he wanted.

Rhys smiled. "Don't change a thing. It's perfect. You did an amazing job."

Scarlett flushed at the compliment. "Do you really like it?"

He grinned. "Absolutely. It's awesome." And he

meant it. Hudson had asked him a while back if he wanted to stick around for Christmas. It seemed like a good idea at the time but, lately, he'd been feeling more like a third wheel. Not enough to go home to see his sisters and their families, but enough to consider going back to work early. He was due back in Jordan at Black Thorn Security on January second. Leave it to Hudson to pick up on that. He owed his friend big time.

Of course Hudson had an ulterior motive. He'd been trying to convince Rhys to stay in Canyon Springs permanently, and he was never one for small measures. This cabin was Hudson's attempt at a bribe, and if Rhys was honest, it was working.

"I'm so happy you like it." Scarlett beamed. She headed into the kitchen area. "I also took the liberty of buying your glasses and dishware. Hudson said you would probably just go out and buy whatever is on sale. I wanted to make sure you had a good set. Oh, and I bought cutlery as well." She opened the cabinets and pulled out a plate so he could see.

Her green eyes sparkled as she spoke. That, paired with her wavy red hair and the slight flush of her cheeks, made her look like a Christmas angel come to life. Rhys laughed. "Hudson is right. I would have bought the cheapest set I could find. So, thank you again. You obviously love what you do. Sunny is very lucky to have you working on the spa project."

Scarlett's face clouded over. "Wellness Retreat.

Yes. Well. That project is not as much fun as this one was." She put the plate back on the shelf.

There it was again—the indication that all was not well with the remodel. Sunny had told him just yesterday that things were going fine and, according to her, they were well on their way to making their opening date of January first, which was just two weeks away. "Why don't you try out your sofa?" Scarlett asked.

Rhys obliged and walked over to the sitting area. He took off his gloves and put them on the table and then he shed his jacket and threw it across the chair. He spotted a peg on the wall and hung his cowboy hat on it. He ran his hands through his thick dark brown hair. Then he sat down on the couch with his long legs stretched out underneath the coffee table in front of him.

The leather was soft under his touch. The cushions were overstuffed so they curled around him and the couch itself was long which was good since he was a little over six feet. He could see lots of naps happening here. "It's great. Very comfortable." He smiled up at her. When she reached down to move the bags out of the way, he spotted a green cushion. "Is that for here as well?"

"Yes. Sorry. I meant to put it on the chair." She leaned over and pulled the cushion out of the bag. "Oh, shit."

"What's wrong?"

"Ah, nothing." She tried to smile, but it looked more like a grimace. "The cushion just has a bit of paint on it." She turned it over so he could see. Sure enough, there was a bright red spot of paint on the back of the pillow. Scarlett tried to stuff it back into the bag, but it wouldn't go in. Clearly off-kilter, she took an awkward step back and hit the coffee table with the back of her legs. She sat down hard on the glass. It didn't shatter, but she swore.

"Are you okay?" Rhys leaned forward so he could help her up.

She nodded but her eyes were bright with unshed tears. Despite her obvious worry about sitting on the glass, she didn't hurry to get up. And the look on her face... She was hurting. He knew a thing or two about that, so he asked, "Seriously, Scarlett, are you okay? It wasn't that hard of a hit, but you seem to be in a lot of pain."

Her face flushed, and she refused to meet his eyes. Almost like she was embarrassed. Huh. Why would she be embarrassed? Unless...from the way she was sitting...was it her ass that hurt? "Ah, sorry. It's none of my business."

Scarlett's flush deepened.

Rhys held up his hands as if to soothe her. "I shouldn't have asked."

"It's... I...fell hard on my butt early this morning. It just hurt when I hit it again."

She wasn't telling him the whole truth. Rhys

knew it wasn't his concern, and yet she seemed like she was in genuine distress. "Are you okay, Scarlett? Do you need help? Is there a boyfriend or someone that's hurting you?" Rhys asked in a quiet voice.

"What? No. No boyfriend. That's not it at all."

"Why don't you tell me what it is like then?"

Scarlett let out a huge sigh. "Someone threw red paint on the walls at the spa this morning. Shit, I mean Wellness Retreat. Even I can't remember to change the name."

Rhys paused for a second. Not what he thought she was going to say, but okay. "What do you mean? Can you explain that a bit more?"

"I headed to the spa at the crack of dawn this morning, and someone came running out as I approached the building. They hit me hard enough to send me flying. I landed on my butt." She cocked her head at him. "Can you break your ass? It sure as hell feels like it's broken."

Rhys grinned. He couldn't help it.

"Anyway, I went inside to check the place over, and the medical center waiting room, which had just been painted a lovely soft gray yesterday, now has red paint all over it. The paint dripped on the new carpet, too." Scarlett took a deep breath, and her shoulders sagged. "The whole room has to be redone."

"I see. Did you see the person who ran you over?"

"No. He wore a balaclava."

"It was a 'he' then?"

"Um, I guess I should say 'they' because honestly, with all the winter clothing it could have been the abominable snowman for all I know."

"What did the police say?"

Scarlett stood up suddenly and winced. "You know what? I don't want to dwell on that part of my day. It was crappy, but this is much better. A happy customer." She walked over and grabbed her coat. "You can keep the green pillow for now. I'll bring you a new one as soon as I get the chance."

"Scarlett, what did Sunny say? Didn't she want to call the police?"

"We talked about it, but we agreed it didn't seem necessary." She was avoiding his gaze again. "I managed to get the guys in, and they replaced the carpet that had paint on it, and they are repainting the walls, so it's all good."

"What about the person who hit you?"

"It was probably some teenager on a dare." She shrugged and tried to smile, but her eyes told a different story. There was fear in them, but she wasn't going to talk to him about it now.

"Why don't we meet for coffee tomorrow morning at the Green Bean Roastery? I'd love to have a chance to say thanks for the great job you did here."

"Ah, well my…"

He knew she would refuse, but he also knew a woman in trouble when he saw one. "I especially like the Christmas tree." He pegged her as a Christmas fan as soon as he saw the coat and boots.

She gave him a real smile this time. "I'm so glad. It's my favorite part, too. Okay, I'll meet you at the Green Bean tomorrow. How's ten?"

"Sounds good." He helped her on with her coat. She grabbed her things and headed toward the door. Rhys followed her. "Do you need help with your stuff?"

"No. I've got it. See you in the morning." She gave him a half-wave and then went out into the cold.

Rhys stood in the doorway, watching Scarlett get into her SUV. His Christmas angel was going to turn into trouble. He knew it in his bones. Was it too late to modify his wish list?

CHAPTER 3

SCARLETT TOOK a sip of her mocha. She hadn't slept much the previous night. Her butt and her back hurt, but the pain wasn't as bad as the fear. She couldn't get the intruder or the damage they'd caused out of her head. Although she wanted to believe it was just some punk kid, what if it wasn't? What if it was someone specifically out to mess with the job...with *her*? She must have gotten up and checked her door twenty times.

Across the table from Rhys, she watched him stir his coffee. Rhys. This man was another reason she'd struggled with sleep. His voice sent shivers down her spine. Did he know he had a soft southern accent on some words? Did he realize what it did to a woman's insides? And that wasn't even factoring in his broad shoulders, his rear end, which was frankly perfect, or those amazing gray eyes that twinkled whenever he smiled. Yes, she'd thought about him in all of those sleepless hours last night.

"Which are your favorite, the gingerbread man, the shortbread cookies, or the double chocolate reindeer brownie?" Rhys asked as he eyed the cookies on the table in front of her.

She looked at the plate. "I don't see a reindeer, just a brownie."

"Use your imagination. I know you have one since you turned that shack into a home for me."

Scarlett smiled. "I do, but I still don't see a reindeer. Maybe a pile of—"

"If you're going to say coal, I'll have to take it back and get you one of the green grinch cookies."

She laughed as she picked up the brownie and broke it into small pieces. "I was going to say a pile of presents before I was so rudely interrupted."

Rhys grinned. "Well, are you going to keep playing with your food, or are you going to eat some? We need to add some more padding to your butt if you're going to keep falling on it."

Scarlett choked on the sip of coffee she'd just taken. Rhys outright laughed. "Sorry, couldn't resist," he said as he winked at her.

She mock glared at him. "I'll remember that. Don't forget, I know where you live."

"So," he said as he dropped the stir stick on the table, "what's the rest of the story?"

Scarlett's heart hammered in her chest. "What are you talking about?"

"You said someone threw red paint on the walls yesterday, but that's not the only thing that's happened."

She licked her lips. "What makes you think that?"

Rhys smiled. "Scarlett, I have five sisters, plus I spent ten years as a Navy SEAL and a few more in the personal protection game. I know when people aren't telling me the whole story. You aren't being completely truthful. Now, I suspect if you knew who pushed you and trashed the reception area, you'd be looking for them rather than sitting here having coffee with me. Which leads me to believe something else is going on."

To stall, Scarlett sipped her mocha and then glanced around the Green Bean. Jenny, the owner, had put up Christmas decorations around the whole shop. Elves and snowflakes sat atop the counter, and garlands wove across the shelves behind it. Christmas carols belted out through the speakers bolted to the ceiling, and the smell of ginger and peppermint filled the air. It felt like they were in a snow globe, but the almost aggressive holiday cheer wasn't getting to her—no, it was the weight of Rhys's gaze that disarmed her.

He stayed silent, watching her, waiting for her to speak. Was this some sort of interrogation technique? She shifted on her chair and winced. Her butt was black and blue, at least the part she could see in the mirror this morning. She set down her mug. "Okay, you're right. There have been more...incidents."

She traced the logo on her coffee cup. "At first, I thought I was just being stupid, you know? But the last couple of things started to make me wonder if something else was going on, and then yesterday..."

Rhys nodded. "Why don't you start at the beginning?"

Scarlett breathed in the sweet, rich scent wafting out from behind the counter as Jenny removed another batch of cookies. She loved the fact Jenny made most of her baked goods. It was one of the reasons the Green Bean Roastery was her favorite café in town. She played with the brownie in front of her as she studied Rhys.

Should she trust this man? There was something in his eyes that made her think she could. Which was why she found herself saying, "During the first week of the job, I set a bunch of stuff down on the counter that used to be just inside the doors. Some folders and my keys on top of it. The contractor was coming, so I headed inside to turn on the lights and make sure everything was ready for him.

When I came back out to the front, the keys weren't on top of my folder anymore. I looked around for them, but then the contractor arrived, and I got busy. An hour or so later, I went back to grab my things, and the keys were sitting on the counter. I figured I'd dropped them and someone had found them and put them back on the desk. I didn't question it much at the time."

Rhys asked, "And you're sure the keys were on top of the folders when you left them there?"

Scarlett hesitated. "I...I thought so, but maybe not. Maybe I did drop them." She broke the stir stick in half. "See? This is why I didn't say anything. It's all so nebulous."

"Tell me what your gut reaction was when you discovered the keys were missing. We are animals, and like all the other animals, our instincts are usually correct. We just sometimes have a hard time following them."

Scarlett froze. It was the kind of thing her mother might have said. Right up until she was murdered.

"Scarlett, are you okay?" Rhys reached out and covered her hand, which lay on the table. Was it *shaking*? She tried to keep her hand still. Concern filled Rhys's sexy gray eyes.

Was she okay? No. Not really. Because it felt like his talk of instincts meant something. Like maybe her mother had somehow managed to send him to her from beyond the grave. She snorted. Or maybe she just needed more sleep. No, what she needed was someone to listen. Someone to help.

"Uh, hi. Scarlett isn't it?" a voice asked.

Scarlett looked up to find two women staring at her. She smiled automatically. "Yes. I'm Scarlett." She searched her memory, but neither of them looked familiar.

"I'm Donna Mercer, and this is Megan West. We both worked at the spa before the renovations."

"Oh, uh nice to meet you." Scarlett shook hands with the women and introduced Rhys. Megan was the taller of the two, a blond in an overstuffed black parka, hair shoved under her hat. Donna was shorter and squatter, her dark hair cropped and her jacket sky blue.

"We were wondering if it's still reopening on schedule in January. We're both hoping to get our old jobs back," Donna said. I know you're the designer, but we thought you'd know about the schedule.

"I was a massage therapist, and Donna was a nurse." Megan smiled. "I got another job, but it's on the other side of Missoula. I won't miss the commute."

"Ah, well, yes, as far as I know, we're on schedule to reopen on January first." Scarlett forced a smile.

"That's great news," Donna said brightly, then her forehead furrowed and she leaned in a bit. "I've heard there were some issues that might delay it."

Scarlett's heart began jackhammering. "No. No delays. It's all good."

"That's a relief." Megan smiled. "I don't know if you remember, but we sort of met before."

Scarlett frowned. "I'm sorry, I—"

"That's okay. We didn't meet so much as I waved

at you. I was with Nathan, that is Dr. Nathan Kyle. We visited the Wellness Retreat about a week ago. Donna was with us."

Donna nodded. "We all banged on the door. We were hoping for a quick tour."

"Oh, right. I remember now." Not that the memory exactly endeared the women to her.

Rhys cocked his head and raised an eyebrow.

Scarlett shrugged. "Last week, these ladies and Dr. Kyle?" She looked at Megan, who nodded. "Banged on the door. Dr. Kyle *really* wanted to see the new facility. He said he would be out of town for the walk-through, and he needed a tour then and there. I apologized, but I told him he would have to clear it with Sunny first."

"Nathan was none too pleased," Megan said. "I tried to explain you were only doing your job, but he's a bit demanding. He says that's what makes him a great surgeon."

Donna covered her snort with a cough, but she winked at Scarlett. Megan frowned. "Anyway, when you wouldn't let him in, he said it was because you were hiding something. He's convinced you're way behind and won't be ready to open on time. I'm so glad he's wrong. I was getting anxious." Her cheeks turned a pale shade of pink.

"Well, we'll leave you to your coffee," Donna said. "Thanks and happy holidays."

"You, too," Scarlett said to the retreating backs of

the two women. She wanted to kill Dr. Kyle for spreading rumors. This was precisely the kind of talk she was so desperate to avoid. If people thought her actions delayed the project significantly, it would spell the end of her interior design career in Canyon Springs. Who wants to hire a designer who causes delays in major projects?

After they left, Rhys just looked at her, his expression making it clear he hadn't forgotten his inquiry. She took a deep breath. "Okay then, yes, my keys were with my stuff. When I came back after doing a walk-through, they were gone. I looked around, but they weren't on the carpet or anywhere else. I was sure someone had taken them."

Rhys brought out a small pad of paper and made some notes. "Go on."

"A week or so later, a set of blueprints went missing. I had them with me. I know I did. They were in this makeshift workspace I was using while on site. Anyway, I went off to make some measurements for some of our installations, but the blueprints were gone when I came back. I didn't spend a ton of time searching, but I did ask the other workers and I checked a few places.

"I had to go to a meeting, and when I got out, I found them tucked under a pile of other papers." She leaned forward and tapped the table with her fingernail for emphasis. "I know they weren't there before the meeting. I *know* it."

A tremor ran down her spine. She must sound like a loon to Rhys, but she prided herself on her organizational skills. As crazy as it sounded it felt like someone was messing with her. If only she knew why.

Rhys's face was hard to read. Did he believe her?

"Okay. What else?"

"Other than yesterday? Nothing. Just the keys and then the blueprints." She took a sip of her now tepid mocha. She glanced at Rhys, and their gazes locked. His eyebrow went up.

"Well...maybe one more thing." She put her cup back down on the table. "This sounds crazy, and I can't believe I'm saying it out loud, but I think I'm being followed."

The air around them suddenly seemed charged. Scarlett frowned as she looked at Rhys. He'd gone completely still. Even his eyes had changed from the warm gray she was used to becoming cold and steely. It was like watching a large cat go from lounging in the sun to stalking its prey. A small frisson of electricity ran across her skin.

"Explain," he growled.

"I, um...it's just a feeling. I didn't see anyone, and nothing was out of place." She shrugged. "Maybe I imagined it."

Rhys leaned over the table, his presence powerful. "I want you to tell me exactly what you felt and when. Don't leave anything out. If you noticed it, no matter if you think it's bizarre or crazy, I want to know."

Scarlett fidgeted with her coffee cup. When Rhys was this close, it was hard to breathe. Those piercing eyes made her feel like he could see down to her deepest, darkest secrets. A rush of heat engulfed her, so she leaned further back in her chair, trying to buy herself some breathing room.

"Sometimes I stay at the Wellness Retreat late, after everyone else has left. One night I was in one of the back rooms by myself, working on some design boards, when…I don't know. It felt like someone was watching me. It… I've never felt it more distinctly. All the hair stood up on my arms and the back of my neck. I looked up, but the doorway was empty and all the windows are covered from the inside. I assumed I was just imagining things, but I couldn't shake the feeling that someone had been there."

Rhys studied her but remained silent.

She swallowed. "It happened again one night outside of my apartment. I looked around, but it was dark, and the parking lot was empty. Still, I was sure someone was there. I didn't know what to do, so I just hustled over to my apartment door and went inside. I made sure I locked everything."

Scarlett glanced at Rhys, but his expression was blank. She put her cup on the table and closed her eyes. It had been a mistake to say anything. She sounded hysterical to her own ears.

The feeling of Rhys's hand descending on hers made her eyes fly open.

"I know it's tough right now. It's hard to trust yourself because you have no tangible proof, and we're always told we need proof we can see, hear, and touch. I believe you. I know you're telling me the truth. Someone is playing games with you."

The tension drained from her shoulders and the knots in her belly unfurled. "Thank you," she whispered, and Rhys squeezed her hand. He had no idea how much his words meant to her. She was beyond exhausted and having someone to confide in who actually believed her was just such a relief.

He leaned back. "So, the question becomes, what are we going to do about it?"

"We?" she asked.

Rhys frowned. "You don't think I'm going to leave you to deal with this on your own, do you?"

"I...that is, I guess I haven't thought about it. I mean, you said we were just coming here so you could buy me coffee as a 'thank you.' I didn't think much beyond that."

Great. Now she sounded like an airhead. She just couldn't seem to get it together in front of this man. And who could blame her? The navy sweater he was wearing gave his gray eyes a slight blue tint and he's shaved his stubble off since yesterday. She like the clean-shaven look even better. His lips were moving, and she was suddenly wondering what it would be like to kiss him. She blinked. She needed to focus on what he was saying with those sexy lips.

"What?" She cleared her throat, trying to ignore the burning of her cheeks. "Sorry, I missed what you were saying."

He studied her, his expression giving nothing away. "I said, the first thing you have to do is tell Sunny everything. Then we—"

"No." She shook her head. "No way."

Rhys frowned. "Why not? She's your boss on this project. She needs to know this morning with the paint wasn't an isolated incident."

Scarlett shook her head once again. "I have worked too hard to build up my business. If people attach me to a project gone wrong, it's over for me. There's no way Sunny can know about the rest of this."

"Sunny isn't like that. She's not going to tank you because someone is screwing with the job. It's not your fault."

"I know *she* won't, but it only takes one rumor for people to decide to go with another interior designer, especially since I'm not a local. I only moved here about eight months ago for a fresh start. Did you hear those women? If there's a delay, they'll blame me. And they'll hate me for it."

Rhys put down his cup. "People won't blame you—"

"You know as well as I do that the rumor circuit

in this town is enough to try and convict someone. Sunny is a local, and even I've heard all about how the people of Canyon Springs were still willing to believe she was responsible for some guy's death. I'm still new here in the town's eyes. One screw up, and I'm done."

She wasn't risking this project. It was her tribute to her mom. Canyon Springs and the spa had been one of her mother's favorite places to come and escape the world. She wanted to honor that. Nothing would get in the way of this being a success.

Rhys cocked his head. "How about this? I'll agree not to say anything unless the danger to you becomes more imminent. But you have to listen to what I say and follow my advice."

Scarlett's eyes narrowed. "What do you mean?"

"I'm going to be your personal security specialist —bodyguard, if you like—until we figure out exactly what you're dealing with and why someone is messing with you."

She started to shake her head again. "No way—"

"It's non-negotiable," Rhys stated in a flat voice. "You either agree to it, or I go to Sunny and spill everything."

"That's not fair! I told you this in confidence," she hissed.

Rhys leaned forward again, resting his elbows on the table. "An unknown subject has been harassing you, spying on you, and following you for weeks.

This is no time to play around. Could it be some idiot with no real ulterior motives? Maybe. But it could also be a stalker and I will not risk your life because you were too worried about your reputation to bring in law enforcement. A career can be fixed. I do not possess the power to bring back the dead."

CHAPTER 4

RHYS LOOKED at the box of cereal in his hand and then at the one on the shelf. For the life of him, he could not figure out the three-dollar price difference. Raisins and flakes were all the same, weren't they? It had been ages since he'd needed to buy groceries on this side of the world. The choices were mind-boggling.

He glanced down at his overflowing cart. Almost like he wasn't leaving soon. Maybe this was stupid. He was only going to be in town for about two more weeks, wasn't he? Wasn't this a lot of trouble for nothing? Or did he want to stay? His gut tied into knots when he thought about leaving, but he assumed it was because he was nervous about going back to work. He glanced at the full cart. Maybe it wasn't. Maybe it *was* because he wanted to stay.

He still hadn't had a chance to talk to Hudson

about the cabin. He'd left a message, but Hudson was out on some job for Hank Patterson and the Brotherhood Protectors, due back today.

Rhys put the box back on the shelf and continued down the aisle.

Truthfully, he *liked* being at the cabin. It really felt like home. It had taken him all of two minutes to move his stuff in last night, mostly because his belongings currently fit into one suitcase. He'd laughed out loud when he'd finally walked into the bedroom and seen the large stuffed camel in the middle of the king-size bed. *A touch of the Middle East*, Scarlett had said when he asked her about it. She'd picked a duvet cover that had a mix of bright reds, blues, and orange to pick up the room since the bed frame was a light wood that matched the floor and the other furniture.

Scarlett. He'd had wicked dreams about her all night. They'd left him horny as hell, but after his chat with her this morning, fear was overriding the sexual tension. Was he really up to the job of protecting Scarlett? The idea that someone was watching her—targeting her—had chilled him to the bone.

His instinct was always to shield women, but with Scarlett, it was something more. Something primal. The moment his gaze had collided with those big green eyes, his protective instinct went into overdrive. The fact that she was in trouble was like adding gasoline to an already raging inferno.

He needed to be on top of his game to keep her safe. The wound in his leg, healed now, seemed to pulse at the very thought of it.

Maybe he should tell Hudson to get one of the Brotherhood guys to come and stay with Scarlett. Yeah, like that was going to happen. Her safety might be a top priority for Rhys, but he wasn't sure the same could be said for another paid protector. No, it had to be him, but was he ready? It was the million-dollar question.

Rhys's cell rang just as he picked up a can of beans. He pulled it out of his pocket and glanced at the screen before answering. "Hudson, I was just gonna call you."

"Are you doing anything important?" Hudson asked. His voice sounded a bit garbled.

"Are you driving?"

"Yes." Hudson's voice broke up but came back clearly a moment later. "Where are you?"

Rhys nudged his cart out of the way for a fellow shopper. "Nowhere important. What's up?"

"Sheriff Striker called. They found a body—the former head of the spa."

"No shit," Rhys said, unceremoniously dumping the can in the cart. His thoughts immediately pinged back to Scarlett and all the trouble she'd been having.

"Yes shit. I'm heading over there now. Want to join me?"

"Absolutely. Text me the address."

"I sent it a few minutes ago before I left."

Rhys glanced down at his phone screen. There was one unread text. "See you shortly." He left the cart in the middle of the aisle and took off for the parking lot. Food would have to wait.

Twenty minutes later, Rhys pulled off the road and parked behind the usual assortment of emergency vehicles. He grabbed his gloves off the seat next to him and slid out of the truck. A chill immediately shot down his spine, reminding him he wasn't in North Carolina. Maybe he was crazy for even remotely considering staying. It was way too fuckin' cold. He did up his coat and plunked the Stetson on his head. He missed his skully, but Hudson had given him the Stetson, so he felt obligated to wear it. He adjusted his sunglasses.

The sky was deep blue, which was nice, but the sun reflected off the snow, making it hard to see. Hard to see and hard to breathe. Why did people live in cold places? And why did Christmas carols make the cold and snow sound so wonderful? He suspected because those singer/songwriters lived out in California, where the prevailing idea was that cold weather was quaint. He'd never understand it. He hated being cold.

He strode toward a cop standing on the other side of a line of yellow tape that cordoned off the road. The man nodded as he approached and lifted the tape for Rhys to go under.

"Aren't you going to ask me for ID or anything?" Rhys asked.

The young cop dropped the tape and hit his gloved hands together, probably so he'd retain feeling in his fingers. "You're Rhys Beckett, aren't you?"

"Yeah."

The cop stomped his feet. "You see anyone else hanging out here freezing their ass off if they don't have to be? It's effing cold. No one is going to wander by this one, believe me."

Rhys nodded and smiled. The cop wasn't wrong. He turned and strode toward a group of men in cold weather gear gathered by the edge of the road, looking down into the trees below.

"Rhys," Sheriff Striker said and offered his gloved hand.

"Striker." Rhys grabbed it, and they shook. There was an unspoken agreement that no one took off their gloves to shake hands when the temperature was hovering in the single digits.

Rhys nodded to Hudson.

"Rhys Beckett," Hudson said and then pointed at the other man in the group, "this is "Stone MacLeod out of the local FBI field office."

Rhys and MacLeod nodded to each other. Then MacLeod's phone rang, and he excused himself from the group to take the call.

"How are you doing, Striker?" Rhys asked.

"Was doing just fine until I got this call." He gestured toward the embankment with his chin.

Rhys took a step and leaned over to see what all the fuss was about. About seventy-five feet down, he could see the back end of a gray car, possibly a Mercedes, sticking out of the snow. The trunk was open, and he could see a glimpse of something inside wrapped in plastic. About twenty feet to the left sat two abandoned snowmobiles.

Striker adjusted his hat as the breeze picked up and blew the top layer of snow in little circles. Sand did the same thing in the desert. "Car was found by a couple of kids out joyriding on snowmobiles. My guys came and popped the trunk, hoping to find a way into the car's front through the back seat. Instead, they found a body wrapped in plastic."

"It's definitely the man who embezzled the money from the Wellness Retreat?" Rhys asked. His gut knotted at the thought of what this might mean for Scarlett. He hadn't been exaggerating earlier—he really did believe in the power of instincts, and his were screaming that her situation had become much more complicated. He thought about telling Striker about her stalker, but he needed to tell Hudson first. They could work on a plan from there.

Striker nodded. "We haven't officially identified him yet, but it's him. Dr. Skipton James Windemere the third. He was the top doc and manager over at the spa. Excuse me, Wellness Retreat."

Rhys cocked an eyebrow. "Skipton Windemere? Seriously?"

Hudson grinned. "Makes you think of butlers and turned-up collars, doesn't it? Maybe his mom is Fifi?"

"Actually, Cecily Banksley-Windemere of the Beverly Hills Banksleys. Or so I'm told." Striker said. "She's called CeeCee for short."

Rhys and Hudson started to laugh. Striker broke into a smile.

"I thought ol' Skippy got out of town a few months ago? Where'd he go?" Hudson asked

Striker pointed. "Right here."

"You mean he's been in the trunk of that car since then?" Rhys asked.

Striker nodded. "Yes."

"How can you be so sure?"

Stone MacLeod rejoined the circle in time to hear the end of their discussion. "We have a description of what he was wearing when he was last seen, and he's still in those clothes. None of his credit cards have been used, nor has any cash been removed from any of his accounts.

"We knew he was supposed to catch a private jet out of Missoula the day he disappeared, but he never showed. The prevailing thought was he changed his mind and decided to flee another way."

Striker shook his head. "Now, it looks like he was killed before he had a chance to make his plane."

Rhys glanced over the side of the embankment again. "Why did no one notice the car before this?"

"Snow." Striker said. "It started snowing just after Halloween and hasn't stopped. This is not a popular area. The nearest house is three miles away. If it hadn't been for those kids out joyriding, he would've been in that trunk 'til spring. Whoever dumped the car had to know that."

Hudson smiled. "Well, now, that tells us something, doesn't it?"

MacLeod nodded. "They had to know he'd be found once the snow melted. The person who did this was buying time."

"Time for what?" Rhys wondered.

"That's the million-dollar question. And did whoever kill him make off with the money from the spa? His personal accounts had a few dollars in them, but we've never recovered the money he embezzled."

All four men looked down the embankment at the body in the trunk. Striker said, "Well no one in the area is spending like they're rolling in cash. Most are strapped with the spa closed for renovation. Local businesses have been grumbling that profits are way down since tourism is down. So if it was a local and they found the money, they're keeping it well hidden."

MacLeod nodded. "Yeah, we've been keeping tabs on the usual players, too. No major changes to the criminal world. All status quo."

Rhys adjusted his cowboy hat. "Do you think the money is still missing then?"

"I wish I knew." MacLeod said. "Striker, I've got to bring my people up to date. I'm pretty sure we'll deal with the money side of things and leave the murder investigation up to you. Keep me updated." He offered his hand, and Striker shook it.

"Will do," the sheriff said. "Let me know if there's anything I should know on your end."

When MacLeod moved off to his SUV, Striker's gaze shifted to Hudson. "I'm gonna need to talk to Sunny about this."

Hudson frowned. "You're not insinuating she—"

"No." Striker shook his head. "But she took over for him. I'm hoping she might be able to shed some light on a few things."

Hudson pulled his cell out of his pocket. "When and where? I'll text her and give her a heads up."

"Ask her if I can drop by either her grandmother's or the Wellness Retreat. I want to go over a few things with her before we take an official statement."

Hudson's fingers flew across the screen.

Rhys stomped his feet a bit. He'd lost feeling in his toes about ten minutes ago. "So, what's the cause of death?"

"As far as we can tell, it looks like someone strangled him, possibly with his laptop bag. It was thrown in the trunk with him. But it also looks like he might have been stabbed as well."

Rhys whistled. "Jesus, someone really wanted him dead."

Striker nodded. "He was a smooth talker, but not much more could be said for him. Went through his share of the family fortune and then some. Screwed around on his wife...and then left her high and dry with a mountain of debt."

"Could it have been the wife?" Rhys asked.

Striker shook his head. "No. Not directly, anyway. She was visiting her family in San Francisco at the time of his disappearance."

Hudson's phone pinged. "Sunny says she can meet you at the spa whenever it's convenient for you." Hudson looked up. "You have her number, right, Striker?"

The sheriff nodded. "Tell her I'll text her a time in a bit. If you boys don't mind, I need to talk to the crime scene people. Get this investigation moving."

Rhys nodded, and Hudson stuck out his hand. "Thanks again for the heads up, Striker. I know Sunny appreciates it as well."

Striker shook hands with both of them. "She already went through hell with that murder investigation. Figured it was the least I could do. You boys take care."

Rhys and Hudson waved at Striker, then started walking back to their cars.

Rhys needed to talk to Hudson about Scarlett and the cabin, but he sure as hell did not want to do it standing outside. "Where are you going now? Do you have time to talk?"

Hudson glanced at him, eyebrow raised. "What's up?"

"Not here." Rhys shook his head. "I don't want to be overheard, and I can't feel my feet."

Hudson laughed. "I forgot you don't like the cold. Let's meet at the house. I could use a cup of coffee."

"I could use at least one. I'm not sure I'll ever feel my toes again."

Hudson grinned. "See you there." He lifted his hand in a wave and hopped into the new pickup he'd bought for his mom. This one was a black Dodge Ram. The last one had come to a bad end after only three weeks. For Hudson's sake, and his mom's, Rhys hoped this one lasted longer. The old gray GMC Hudson had lent him didn't have any bells and whistles, but it drove, which was all he had needed, and it had a working heater, which he cranked to the highest setting possible.

Thirty minutes later, Rhys hit the button on the built-in coffee maker in the ranch's kitchen. He flexed his thawing toes. "I don't know how you do it. Better yet, why?"

"Why what?" Hudson asked, then took a sip of coffee.

"Choose to live somewhere where you could actually lose body parts because of the weather." The coffee maker dinged to announce it had done its thing. Rhys grabbed the mug and took a sip. The warmth from the hot drink filtered to his feet, or at least that's what it felt like. He was gaining a better appreciation of warm drinks now that he lived in a place where it routinely hit single digits.

Hudson laughed. "You've spent time in the cold before. Winter in Afghanistan is no joke. It's cold in those mountains."

"True, but that's war. I went where I was told. You *chose* to live here." He looked down and wriggled his toes again inside his wool socks. "It's inhuman." He crossed the kitchen with his coffee, then sat down across the table from Hudson.

"It's how I grew up. I don't think about it much." Rhys shot him a disbelieving look, and Hudson laughed. "Okay, I notice it a lot more now that I'm not a kid, but it's home, and Sunny's grandmother is here, so it is what it is."

"I still think you're crazy." Rhys reached out and grabbed a warm chocolate chip cookie off the plate that was sitting on the table between them. "I love cleaning day. Martha makes the best cookies."

Hudson nodded. "She does. Don't worry, she'll make you cookies, too, when she comes to clean your place."

Rhys leaned back. "I need to talk to you about that." He took a breath and swallowed the slight lump that was building in his throat. "Hudson, I appreciate what you did for me. Getting Scarlett to fix up that old cabin." He paused and swallowed again. "That was something else. I—"

"I did it for me," Hudson said.

Rhys frowned. "What do you mean? I'm sorry if I've been crowding you and Sunny. All you had to do was tell me, you know that. I can find a place in town...or, hell, I can go back to the Middle East early. I'm about ready."

"No! No. That's not what I meant at all. I did it so you'd stay." Hudson leaned back in his chair and assessed his friend. "Cards on the table time. I don't want you to go back and work for Black Thorn." He raised a hand as if anticipating an objection. "Not because I don't think you're ready. Your leg is fine. I'm happy the bullet didn't leave any permanent damage.

"I want you to stay here because I want you to work with me. Hank Patterson has built something special here, and although I've only been working with him for a couple of months, it's clear to me this is where I want to be. I'm with the woman I love, doing a job I love. I think I'm truly happy for the first time in...forever."

Rhys took another sip of coffee. "I'm glad that you're happy, man. You deserve it, but I'm not sure this is my thing." He was tempted to stay, even with the cold which he absolutely hated, far more than he thought possible. That niggling fear in the back of his mind wouldn't let him. He thought about sharing his doubts with Hudson—his fear that he might have lost his edge and his conviction that he would only know if he went back to the place where he'd been shot.

Hudson smiled. "I am. That's what I'm talking about." He leaned forward again. "How long have we known each other? Ten years or so?"

"Give or take."

"And in that time, we've always had each other's backs. Hell, that bullet you took saved my ass." He gave him an intent look. "I know you like I know myself. You'll enjoy working for Patterson. He and his people know their shit, and they've got all the bells and whistles that make the work easier. Think about it. You get to do the job you love here instead of halfway around the world, and you get to do it with people who get you."

Hudson scratched the stubble on his chin. "All I'm saying is I know you well enough to know you'll like the work and the people. You can have a home here if you want it." He smirked. "If you can take the cold."

Rhys nodded and jammed another cookie in his mouth because he just didn't know what to say. Hudson was right. His friend knew what he really wanted. A home. A place of rest. Somewhere he could be free of his sisters' drama, but close enough to take a short plane ride to visit them if he liked. After their mother passed away, they'd all started smothering him. He'd lost one mother and gained five new ones.

Hudson was watching him. "Just promise me you'll think about it."

"I'll think about it." That, at least, was something he could promise. "But whatever happens, I'm seriously grateful for the place. It means a lot."

Hudson smiled. "So, what's so important you couldn't talk about it in front of Striker?"

Rhys sighed. He'd made a promise to Scarlett only a couple of hours ago, and already he was breaking it. Finding that dead body had changed everything. His stomach clenched, but he forged ahead.

"Scarlett and I had coffee this morning at the Green Bean Roastery."

"Mmm-hmmm." Hudson started to smile.

"Stop. It wasn't like that." At least not yet. *Focus*. "I noticed she was in pain."

Hudson's brow immediately furrowed. "Why? Did someone hurt her?"

"I take it she didn't tell you that the person who threw the red paint on the walls sent her flying when they ran out of the building?" He'd suspected as much given her reaction to the thought of telling Sunny about the stalker.

"No. Scarlett said the perp flew by her."

"Yeah, well, they knocked her flat on her ass, and she's bruised up."

Hudson shook his head. "That's not good. She should have mentioned it."

Rhys made a silent apology to Scarlett before he

continued. "There are a lot of things she didn't mention that she should have." He went on to outline what was going on, ending with, "So, she didn't say anything because she thinks this is a make or break project for her. She's worried the town will turn on her, like what happened with Sunny, if the reopening stalls."

Hudson grimaced. "Son of a bitch." He shook his head. "She still should've said something."

"Probably, but would you in her shoes? Better yet, would Sunny?"

"No. You're right. Sunny wouldn't." Hudson got up and went over to the coffee machine and hit the button. The machine started its whirring and grinding. It was kind of annoying that it didn't make a pot just a single cup. On the other hand the coffee was always fresh.

"What do you think is going on?"

Rhys shrugged. "Truth be told, this morning I was thinking someone was just trying to harass Scarlett. Maybe a competitor or a pissed-off ex, but it feels a whole lot more sinister now that the former manager's body showed up."

"Agreed. Chances are good it's not a competitor trying to ruin Scarlett's reputation. We can't totally rule it out, but still, I'm with you. So what do you want to do about it? I've got another job this week, but I can try and switch with one of the other Brotherhood guys."

Rhys shook his head. "No, I've got this. I promised her I would keep an eye on her and help out."

Hudson cocked an eyebrow at him. "Oh, really? You're going to take the job?"

"Yes. I already said I would." God help him. He'd better be up for it.

Hudson grabbed his coffee and sat back down at the table. "And you aren't going to enjoy this job at all, are you? Having to stay by the beautiful and talented Scarlett's side day. *And* night?" Hudson laughed. "It's going to be a tough one."

Hudson was right. Scarlett was beautiful and talented. Not to mention, she had an amazing ass. Rhys grinned. "Someone has to do it."

CHAPTER 5

SCARLETT TOOK a deep breath and let it out slowly. She'd tried all her relaxation techniques to keep from killing Rhys, but none of them were working. Not even Bing Crosby singing about a white Christmas was helping.

She glared at him across her kitchen table. "How could you? You sat there in the cafe and promised me you wouldn't say anything. It hasn't even been half a day! Is something wrong with your short-term memory?"

Rhys frowned. "I understand you're upset, but if you remember, I actually said I wouldn't say anything unless the danger escalated. Scarlett, things are completely different now, and people need to know what's going on to handle it properly."

"Bullshit! How much danger can I be in? Whoever's messing with me is a creep, but the worst they've done is ruin a new paint job." She stood up and started pacing back and forth. "I shouldn't have told you in the first place! If there's an investigation into the stuff that's been happening to me, it might cause a delay in the reopening and people are going to be pissed."

She turned to face Rhys. "I'm going to be a pariah. I'll never get my new business off the ground. I might as well throw in the towel now. People are counting on it opening back up by the new year. They need those jobs, and they need the tourists to come back and spend money in their shops and restaurants."

"I hear what you're saying," Rhys said in a calm voice, "but people will have other things to gossip about, believe me."

"What could be bigger gossip in this town than the spa not opening on time?" Scarlett demanded.

"A dead body found in a trunk."

Scarlett froze mid-step. She blinked. "What? There's a dead body?"

"Yes."

Scarlett slowly lowered onto her chair. "In a trunk? Who? Where?" She shook her head. "I can't believe— What is going on?"

Rhys got up and grabbed the coffee pot off the counter. He came back and filled Scarlett's mug, then put the pot back and brought out the milk. Scarlett fixed up her coffee the way she liked it and took a sip.

Then another. "Wait. How did you know I needed...a minute?"

"Like I said. Five sisters. I recognized the signs."

Scarlett blinked. "Okay. I'm ready. Explain."

"After I left you, I got a call from Hudson. They found Dr. Windemere out on Fulsom Road. He'd been strangled and possibly stabbed and was then wrapped in plastic and stuffed in the trunk of a car that had been pushed off the side into the ravine below."

"Wait. Is Windemere the former manager of the spa? The one who embezzled all the money?

Rhys nodded.

Scarlett took another sip of coffee and tried to let it all sink in.

Rhys moved the poinsettia that was in the middle of the table to the side and then leaned forward. "Scarlett, I wouldn't have broken your confidence, but I think you can understand how this changes things. The dead man embezzled money from the spa you're working on reopening. I have no idea what the connection is to what's going on with you, but I'm sure there is one. That's why I told Hudson. Sunny needs to know from a business perspective but also for her own safety. I'm quite sure she and Hudson told Sheriff Striker as well.

"Hey, I know you're worried," he said in a softer voice. "I didn't want to break your confidence, but this was the right call. It's safer for everyone to know what's going on. Sunny wants to talk to you. Today, if you're willing. I know it's your day off, but all things considered..."

Scarlett leaned back in her chair and wiped her palms on her jeans. She tried to let Dean Martin singing about chestnuts and Jack Frost soothe her jangling nerves. She reached for a gingerbread man from the plate of cookies on the table. After biting off his leg, she chewed slowly, letting the gingery flavor linger in her mouth.

Well, shit. Rhys was right. The dead body changed things. The gingerbread sat heavily in her belly. She wanted so badly to make this project work.

The old spa had been one of her mother's favorite places. It was her escape from L.A. and the fame she'd found there. People treated her like a normal human when she was here. No one asked her about her secret ingredients or how to cook anything, and her mother had loved the locals so much for it.

She'd had so many ideas about how it could be improved...ideas Scarlett had integrated into her designs wherever possible. It was her way of helping her mom make a difference even now when she wasn't here anymore. But it might have all been for nothing. She was going to have to apologize to Sunny for keeping her in the dark. Would Sunny fire her? She found herself tapping the cookie in her hand to the beat of "Jingle Bells."

"Does Sunny like gingerbread?" Maybe she could

bribe her with cookies. Everyone loved cookies, right?

Rhys chuckled. "I have no idea, but I do." He took another cookie, his fourth since he'd sat down, and bit off its head.

"Okay, let me pack up an assortment of Christmas cookies, and we'll head over to the Wellness Retreat, or wherever Sunny wants to meet."

"The spa is fine. She's already over there working on some stuff. Hudson's with her."

Scarlett got up and went to her cupboard. She got out a cookie tin that had a snowman on it and took it over to the counter where she filled it with an assortment of holiday cookies she'd baked earlier. "Okay," she said as she put the cover on the tin, "let's go face the music."

Hoping the cookies would afford her a little holiday magic, she put on her coat and collected her things. Rhys got up, pulled on his coat, and hurried to get the door for her. "I *am* sorry, Scarlett, but I won't let anyone get hurt if it can be avoided."

Scarlett wasn't happy about any of this, but she could see Rhys's point. Sighing, she followed him out the door, locked up, and joined him in his old pickup. The whole time, her mind was whirring through different scenarios. She was going to fall all over herself apologizing to Sunny, and then she would beg to keep this job. She would even tell the truth about her mother if she had to. This job was too important for her to lose.

They pulled up in front of the spa, and Scarlett gathered her things. The ride over had been mostly silent. Rhys had seemed to understand her need for quiet reflection, and he'd left her to her machinations. It amazed her, actually, that he hadn't attempted to force the issue. She didn't know him well, but she already felt comfortable around him, so much that the silence seemed normal. He was good at reading her moods and her needs. Maybe it was having all those sisters. Perhaps he did understand women.

Rhys grabbed the tote she'd brought, and they walked over to the door. When she wobbled on the ice, he glanced down at her spike-heeled boots. She prepared for the comment she knew was coming, but he remained silent. Further evidence of Rhys's superpower—his understanding of the female mind. Or more likely, a well-developed sense of survival. That's probably what he'd learned from having five sisters: how to keep his mouth shut. Scarlett smiled.

"You're smiling like you just figured out a big secret," Rhys commented. "Care to share?"

Scarlett laughed as she opened the door to the spa. "I did figure out a secret but, no, I'll keep this one to myself." She walked across the lobby to set her coat and purse down on the desk, and Rhys mimicked her, only with his coat and her tote.

Scarlett heard Sunny's voice coming from the hallway. She took a deep breath and tried to calm her heartbeat. It was like being called to the principal's office.

Rhys reached out and squeezed her arm. "You're fine," he said in a soft voice as Sunny and Hudson came into view.

"Scarlett," Sunny said as she hurried across the foyer. "I am so sorry. What a nightmare." She reached for her, pulling her into a hug.

Scarlett was caught entirely off guard. She'd expected a lecture or an evisceration. Not a hug. "Um, thanks," she said as she hugged Sunny back.

Sunny released her and stepped back to lean into Hudson's arm. "It's chilly in here." She shivered.

Scarlett silently cursed herself. "The guys brought in some equipment earlier, so they kept the doors propped open for a while. Ben, the lead contractor, sent me a text to let me know in case the guys were painting today. Sorry, I should have let you know." She was screwing up all over the place. "Look, Sunny, I know I should've told you everything earlier—"

"Yes, you should have. I don't want anyone on this project to feel unsafe." She put a hand on Scarlett's arm. "I hate that you thought you had to go through this alone. But I totally understand why you didn't say anything. This town can be...tough on people. I know you're just starting out here, and if people turn on you, it feels like there's no coming back."

Scarlett swallowed the lump of tears in her throat and nodded.

Sunny smiled. "I understand. Completely. Just so you know, you can count on me to have your back. If this project falls apart somehow, that's on me. It's my job to take the heat. I hired you because I believe in your talent. You're the best one for this job."

Scarlett couldn't breathe. No client had ever been this nice to her. She blinked hard to hold back the tears. If she started crying, Sunny might change her mind and decide she was a lunatic after all. "I— Thank you. That means more than I can say." Her voice caught so she swallowed. "I promise I won't keep anything else from you, and I will do my utmost to make sure my part of the project comes together on time."

Sunny smiled. "I know you will. I have no doubts."

Rhys suddenly nudged Scarlett's elbow. She looked down at the table. The snowman tin in the tote smiled up at her. "Oh"—she grabbed the tin —"these are for you." She handed it over.

Sunny immediately opened it. "Oh, these look and smell wonderful." Her eyes lit up, and she placed the tin and cover on the counter and grabbed a ginger-bread man. She took a bite and closed her eyes. "These are divine. Did you make these? Oh, my God, Hudson, you have to have one."

When Hudson reached for a cookie, Sunny suddenly snatched the tin away so quickly the cookies almost spilled out. "No. Wait. If you eat one, you won't stop, and I won't have any cookies left. I lied. They're horrible. You won't like them." She held the cookies as far above her head as she could, which was laughably insufficient given his greater height.

Hudson shook his head. "See what I have to put up with? Come on. One cookie."

Sunny's eyes narrowed. "Okay, but only because you promised to fix the leak in Gran's bathroom." She brought the tin back down. Hudson swooped in quickly and grabbed a sugar cookie decorated like a Christmas present.

"These *are* good," he said through a mouthful of cookie. He reached for a second one.

"One. That's it. No more for you!" Sunny slammed the cover back on the tin.

Scarlett burst out laughing. It was great to see this playful side of Sunny. It made her feel like they could be friends rather than just colleagues, and Scarlett desperately needed a friend right now. "Don't worry, Sunny, I love baking. If Hudson eats them all, I'll make you more. Tell me your favorite kinds."

"See, she'll make you more cookies. Your favorites." Hudson reached for the tin.

"Touch it and die, buddy." Sunny said it with a scowl but relented in the next breath. "One more, but that's it."

Hudson nodded as he opened the tin and grabbed a gingerbread man. He held the cookie between his teeth as he closed the container and scooped it off the counter. When the cookie emerged, it lacked a head. "Yup, let's go." He turned and started walking toward the door with the cookie tin tucked under his arm.

"Wait," Sunny yelled. She grabbed her coat and purse and then turned and gave Scarlett a quick hug. "Hang in there, and don't worry about all this. We'll get it sorted out."

"Thank you, Sunny. I can't tell you how much I appreciate your understanding."

Sunny waved a hand in the air. "Don't give it another thought. We'll talk tomorrow." She turned and marched after Hudson.

"Hudson Riggs, if you eat another cookie, I will—"

Sunny let go of the door, so Scarlett didn't hear the end of the threat. She had a feeling it would be a good one. She made a mental note to ask Sunny the next time she saw her.

"So"—she turned to Rhys—"I guess this is where I say you were right. I should have told her a long time ago."

Rhys looked at her and smiled. "This is where you give me a tour of the place. I want to see the changes you've made."

"That's right, Hudson mentioned you used to come here. Did you ever use the spa facilities?"

Rhys shook his head. "Just the medical side of

things. I saw one of the doctors. She did a great job with my leg."

Scarlett didn't pry. She'd heard Rhys had gotten shot overseas, but he was fairly direct when he wanted to be—if he felt like talking about it, he would have mentioned it. So she wasn't about to bring it up. Everyone had things they didn't want to talk about...and she was no exception.

"Well, come on. I'll give you the grand tour, but you'll have to use your imagination in parts because it's not finished yet."

Rhys's voice took on a husky tone. "I'm pretty good with my imagination, so bring it on."

Scarlett looked up at him. His gray eyes were twinkling. Heat spread across her cheeks. There was no doubt what he was referring to. Damn, if this man didn't make her forget what she was saying. She was starting to feel hot in other ways. Maybe understanding the female mind wasn't his only superpower.

CHAPTER 6

"So that's it. What do you think?" Scarlett asked, her eyes sparkling with pride.

It lifted Rhys's spirit to see her in her element. He liked this confident, strong Scarlett, the same one who'd showed him the cabin the other day. Seeing the fear in her eyes earlier, it had almost been too much to bear. He'd wanted to throat-punch the people who'd made her feel that way.

"It's amazing," he said simply. Because it was true. He wished he could tell her the truth: she was amazing, too.

Her cheeks colored, something that seemed to happen every five minutes, and she looked down at the counter.

"No, really. I was here before. It was nice, but it had a clinical feel. The patient rooms were just like they were at my regular doctor's. I sat on a table with the kind of paper that crinkles every time you move, wearing a paper gown. They tried to fancy it up with better paint colors and nice lighting, but let me tell you, I was very aware I was seeing a doctor."

She reached out and squeezed his arm. "Thanks. That means a lot. I spent a lot of time talking to some of the former medical staff here, asking what their dream exam rooms would look like. Seeing the doctor can be a scary and challenging experience. I wanted to eliminate that if I could."

"Your paint and lighting are great, but it's the beds that will make the difference. No crappy foam. But the massage beds with real blankets. It's so much more comfortable. I like your idea of the patients wearing spa robes as well. It's more..." He struggled for the right word. "Protective? No man is comfortable in a paper gown. The robes will make people feel less vulnerable. I know people will appreciate being treated like human beings. It's more...welcoming. Less intimidating."

Scarlett scoffed. "You? Intimidated? I don't believe it."

Rhys leaned against the counter. "Scarlett, when you're sick or in pain and you have to go see a doctor who holds your future in their hands, it's terrifying and intimidating as hell, no matter who you are."

"Oh...I didn't mean to insult you." Color rose in her cheeks, and she bit her lower lip. "I—"

"It's okay, no insult taken. I think you've done a

great job here, and the patients who walk through those doors are going to feel less anxious because of your changes. You should be proud of yourself. You're making a difference."

"Thanks." Scarlett's smile turned mischievous. "I think I'd like to see you in one of those paper gowns. The kind with the patterns. Maybe kittens! And pink, to bring out your skin tone."

Rhys snorted. His eyes locked with Scarlett's, and desire shot through his veins. This woman stoked fires in him like no other woman ever had before. But this was not the time or the place, and Scarlett was now a client of sorts. He had to focus on bringing his A-game. *If it still exists.*

Rhys swallowed hard and broke eye contact. He glanced down at the desk behind the counter. There was a stuffed animal lying there. "What's that?"

Scarlett laughed as she reached over and picked up the stuffed toy. "That's Montana Moose."

There it was again. The sense that Scarlett was familiar somehow. Something about her laugh, or her smile maybe? Rhys shrugged off the thought. He would have remembered if he'd met her before. "Does someone bring their kids here?"

"No. Andy, the painter, found him in here after everything was cleared out, and we decided to use him as our mascot. Every day, Montana Moose finds another place to sit and watch the progress, sort of like the Elf on the Shelf. You know, the little doll parents move around the house to convince the kids he's reporting back to Santa about their behavior."

Rhys raised an eyebrow. "Who does Andy believe the moose is reporting to?"

Scarlett ran her fingers over the stitches on the Moose's back and fluffed up Montana Moose's fur. Then she straightened his antlers. "Me. He jokes that Montana is my proxy, keeping an eye on him and making sure everything goes according to plan."

"I see." The guy had a thing for Scarlett. Noted. Maybe he was the one messing with her. Could be he wanted the job to last longer. Keeping that thought to himself was best at the moment. He didn't want Scarlett to have to look at her coworkers with suspicion just yet.

"He has another purpose, too. The moose, that is."
"What's that?"

"Andy always puts the moose on the desk behind the counter when he leaves. It makes life easier for both of us. He doesn't have to find me to let me know he's leaving, and I don't have to search to make sure he's gone."

Rhys froze for just a second. Not good. She clearly trusted Andy, and maybe she was right to, but if not, the guy had found the perfect way to get her to leave him unsupervised in the building site.

Her smile slipped. "Everything okay?" Scarlett asked.

Shit. Rhys didn't want her to freak her out unnecessarily. She was already close to her breaking point. He'd noticed her tapping that cookie earlier. "All good. What do you say we do a quick sweep and then head out, maybe grab some dinner?"

"Um, sure, but if the moose is here, Andy and his people are gone. We don't need to."

"Humor me," Rhys said as he stood up straight. "We'll start at the back and work our way forward."

Scarlett shrugged but gamely led the way to the back of the building. Rhys was a step or two behind. He wanted to make mental notes so he could memorize the layout.

Scarlett's scent, a mix of citrus and ginger, was very distracting. Of course, walking behind her was even more distracting. He kept glancing at her butt as they made their way down the hall. Might as well enjoy his work as much as he could. Soon enough, he'd be back in the Middle East, doing protection jobs for top business execs who invariably were assholes.

About fifteen minutes later, after a short bathroom break, they were back at the front of the building. "Happy?" Scarlett asked.

Rhys smiled. "Sure. Where should we go for dinner?"

Scarlett glanced at her watch. "I had no idea it was that late. Um, I can't believe I'm saying this because I usually love getting dinner out, but I'm exhausted. It's been a bit of a roller-coaster day, and truth be told, my back is really starting to hurt."

Rhys immediately kicked himself for having made her do a full walk-through of the spa again. "Let's get you home then." They both put on their coats, Rhys holding hers up for her, which earned him a smile, and headed for the door. Before she walked out, he motioned for her to stand back so he could go first. He glanced around the lot. It was empty. He left the building, followed by Scarlett, who locked the door behind them.

Rhys's muscles stiffened and not just from the cold. Darkness had descended, making the temperature plummet further. "I will never get used to how cold it gets here."

Scarlett nodded. "I know what you mean. I expected it to be cold, but not like this. The songs lie to people."

"Songs?"

"Christmas music. All that nonsense about letting it snow and sleigh riding. They make it sound fun, but it's miserable."

"I agree. It's just flat-out lying." They arrived at the old pickup, and Rhys quickly went around and opened the door for Scarlett. "Don't worry, I'll get you warmed up in no time." He reached down and took the stuff from her, tucking it behind her seat in the king cab. When he glanced back at Scarlett, her cheeks had a pink tint. He frowned, thinking back on what he'd said, and then his face split in a grin.

Scarlett gave him the side-eye as she climbed up into the truck's passenger side. "Careful there, cowboy, or no more cookies for you."

Rhys closed the door behind her, chuckling all the way around to the driver's side. It didn't take much to get her going. He liked that. Her frequent blushes only made her cuter. He climbed in the driver's side and turned over the engine. Within minutes, the old truck was cranking out heat. Scarlett's eyelids started to droop, and a few minutes later, she was asleep.

The drive to her place was short, but he let her rest. God only knew what time she'd crawled out of bed this morning. It had been a long, emotional day for her. He wondered if he should stop and get her something to eat but decided against it. She was a grown woman, and if her cookies were anything to go by, she knew her way around the kitchen. He didn't want to overstep.

Two minutes later, he pulled into the side parking lot next to her little apartment house. He didn't love that she was on the ground floor or that her unit was accessible from outside. It would have been better if there were a lobby or at least a set of double security doors, but the door faced the parking lot only and wasn't directly on the street. The lot was well lit, cutting down on the risk factor.

He leaned over and gently shook Scarlett. "Hey, you're home."

She blinked and looked around. "Oh, I guess I fell asleep."

"You're exhausted, and I imagine you haven't been getting much sleep lately. Tonight you can. The secret is out, and no one thinks it's your fault."

Scarlett looked at him and smiled. It felt like a gut punch when he saw the undisguised relief in her eyes. She blinked rapidly. "You were right...about telling Sunny. Thank you." They got out of the truck silently, Scarlett sliding out before Rhys could come around and open the door for her. Together, they started toward her apartment. Rhys's step faltered, and he tugged her arm. Well-honed security instincts prickled along his spine. "Scarlett, go back and get in the truck." He pulled the keys from his front pocket and forced them into her hand.

"What? Why?" Scarlett blinked. "What's going on?"

"Just get in the truck. Driver's side. Start it and have 911 ready to go on your phone."

"Rhys, you're scaring me," she said in a soft, thready voice. "What's wrong?"

Rhys swore a blue streak in his head. She needed to listen to him now. "Scarlett. The outside light is off. It was on when we left. You need to get in the truck, start it, and have 911 teed up on your phone. I'm going over to check it out. If I don't come out within two minutes, hit 911, and leave. Drive back to the gas station we passed. It's two blocks over. Sit there and wait."

She was already shaking her head. "I'm not leaving you here."

"Scarlett!" It came out harsher than intended, but she needed to understand she could be in danger. "Just get in the truck," he gritted out between clenched teeth.

Her face flushed, and anger flashed in her eyes before she turned on her heels and stalked to the truck. She started to get in but turned back. "The keys to my place," she said as she moved in his direction.

"The door is already open."

She froze. Then she glanced at the door, cracked slightly open.

"Truck. Now!" Rhys growled.

Scarlett gave him no argument this time. She made a beeline back to the truck, hopped in, and had it going before the door closed. Thank God. Rhys turned toward her place and crept toward the door, scanning the surrounding area as he went. His instincts told him he was alone, but he stayed alert. He'd gotten distracted before. His leg chose this moment to twinge as a reminder of what happened when he lost focus.

Someone had used a wedge of some sort to force the door. They'd damaged the frame, so it hadn't been silent. He glanced around again. It wouldn't have made a tremendous amount of noise, either. Still the intruder had clearly thought it was worth the risk. Noted.

Rhys didn't want to be framed in the doorway with the ambient light behind him. It would make him a target. Instead, he leaned his back against the building and pushed the door open with his right hand.

He dropped low and entered. A quick scan of Scarlett's main living area revealed chaos. The kind that told him the rest of the place would be trashed as well. He let his senses register the whole room and then moved beyond it. The place was empty. He knew it in his bones. All those years in the military and doing security work had honed his skills to knife-edge sharpness, and the months he'd spent in recovery hadn't robbed him of anything.

He slowly stood, letting out a breath as he did. It was a great relief to know his instincts were still there. Now was his focus still on point? Could he still manage in a fire fight or a hostage situation? He'd have to go back to work to find out for sure.

Rhys needed to search the place anyway just to be safe. He reached into one of the cargo pockets in his coat and pulled out the mini Maglite he never left home without, using the sparse light it cast to pick his way across the floor. He didn't want to contaminate the scene any more than he had to.

Scarlett was going to lose it when she saw her place. Nothing was untouched. The intruder had slashed couch cushions and pillows. Stuffing covered the surfaces like tufts of snow, and the contents from the overturned coffee table and the end tables were strewn everywhere. Broken picture frames had been left in a pile—the pictures themselves were all over.

The kitchen was more of the same. Dry goods covered every surface. Cereals and flour coated the counters and the floor. The kitchen table had been turned over along with the chairs. The open freezer door was dripping melted ice cream onto the mat that used to be by the kitchen sink.

Rhys continued through the rest of the apartment. The bathroom and the bedroom were both destroyed. Either someone had been desperate to find something, or the perp had it in for Scarlett. He sincerely hoped it was the former, because if the person who'd done this had been driven by spite, Rhys wasn't too sure they were sane. And that terrified him. A shiver went across his skin, and the hair on the back of his neck stood up.

His walk-through complete, Rhys made a quick exit and emerged from her front door. He strode quickly to the truck. Scarlett's face was pale in the darkness. She rolled down the window.

"Call 911," he said.

"What is it? What's going on?" Her eyes were huge, and her hands shook as they held the phone.

"Someone broke in. It looks like they were searching for something. They're gone, but Scarlett"—Rhys grimaced—"your place..."

"What? What about it?" she demanded.

Rhys sighed. "There's a lot of damage. I'm so sorry." He hadn't thought she could get any paler, but her skin turned the color of newly fallen snow as she glanced at the apartment's darkened doorway. She swayed a bit in her seat, and he reached through the window and grabbed her shoulder to steady her. "Scarlett." He gave her a little shake. She blinked as if struggling to focus, and panic mounted in his gut. Was she going into shock?

"I'm all right," she said in a quiet voice.

Rhys stepped back and opened the truck door. He took the phone out of Scarlett's hand and hit the call button.

"911. What's your emergency?"

Rhys explained the situation in detail and then hung up and dialed Hudson. After filling him in, he hung up and handed the phone back to Scarlett. She was still deathly pale. He held on to her shoulder and purposely blocked her view of her place. "Help is on the way."

"I want to see it," she said in a small voice.

"You can't right now."

"Rhys, I need to see it." Her voice was firmer. Although she was still pale, her eyes were clear and focused.

Rhys said a silent prayer of thanks. "I know, honey, but you can't go in until the cops get here. It's a crime scene. They need to process it before you can get back in."

Scarlett's eyes narrowed, but after a second, she gave a slight nod. "Fine. But I want to see it as soon as they're finished."

Rhys nodded. He was already trying to figure out how to soften the blow, but he'd been around the block enough to know nothing would. Sirens approached from the distance, and a few minutes later, the area was lit up with flashing lights. Three cop cars parked haphazardly in the parking lot. The officers all jumped out and started toward the apartment. Rhys stepped away from the truck, shutting the door behind him, and approached them with his hands held in plain sight. "I'm the one who called 911."

"You're Rhys?" the first officer asked.

"Yeah."

"What's going on?"

The other officers joined the first, and they formed a huddle against the cold while Rhys explained the situation. After he finished, one of the cops—Officer Jenkins, according to his name tag— stepped forward and started giving directions to the rest. Rhys headed back to the truck, but he didn't open the door this time. It was cold, and she needed to be kept warm.

If he had his way, he'd send her to the hospital to get checked out. She was in shock, or near enough. But she'd never agree. Funny, he'd known her for all of a day, but he already knew her. Or at least it felt like he did.

The sound of crunching gravel reached his ears. Rhys turned and saw Hudson and Sheriff Striker walking toward him. Hudson was holding two to-go cups. "As discussed. This one"—he put his right hand forward—"is hot chocolate. Extra hot and sweet. He handed the second cup to Rhys. "This is your coffee."

"Thanks," Rhys said. He'd made the request because Scarlett needed the heat and the sugar. With any luck, it would help snap her out of the shock she seemed to be locked in. "Give me a sec to give this to Scarlett, and I'll come back and fill you in." He turned around and headed back to the door of the truck. Scarlett looked up and rolled down the window.

"Here." He handed her the hot chocolate. "It's still hot. Be careful. It's also extra sweet. You may not like the taste, but it will help you feel less...unsteady."

Scarlett nodded and took the cup.

"I'm going over to speak with Hudson and Sheriff Striker. I'll be back in a few minutes. Yell if you need anything." He turned to walk away.

"Rhys?"

He came back to the window.

"This is serious, isn't it?"

Rhys hesitated but then nodded. She needed to know the truth.

"Thank you," Scarlett said with a tight smile. "I appreciate that you didn't lie to me. I would prefer to know the truth. Always."

Rhys reached in the truck and squeezed her arm. Then turned and made his way over to Hudson and Striker.

"How is she?" Hudson asked in an undertone.

"Scared. And shaken. It's all just sinking in. I think she half convinced herself the other stuff wasn't real."

Hudson nodded. "Whoever did this started out small, probably to keep her guessing. No one wants to think they're being targeted."

"Agreed. But she is being targeted. Sunny and Hudson filled me in on everything this afternoon," Striker said.

"Bill Striker." The local police chief, Fred Wells, approached the group with a bit of a swagger, which more closely resembled a waddle since he was over-weight and dressed in a black down jacket with a white sweater on underneath. He reminded Rhys of a penguin. "This is a bit outside of your turf. What are you doing here?"

Striker nodded. "Chief Wells. There might be an overlap with one of my cases. Thought I'd come check it out."

The chief gave Hudson and Rhys a once-over and then ignored them. "I heard you found yourself a body today. The head doc from the spa. That's gonna be messy. You think it's connected to this break-in? Why?"

Striker leaned against the back of Rhys's pickup truck. "Ms. Jones works at the spa."

The chief snorted. "She's some kinda decorator girl. She wasn't working at the spa when the doc disappeared. She's got nothing to do with it."

Rhys's hackles rose. "Interior designer."

Wells grunted. "Whatever you want to call it. If this is your big break, you're in big trouble, Striker. You're already grasping at straws."

Striker gave the chief a quick smile but refused to rise to the bait. Hudson and Rhys remained silent. They knew from experience the chief preferred quick and easy answers to the truth. It was why he'd arrested Sunny for a murder she didn't commit. It was why he'd ignored all the signs that one of his deputies was crooked.

The chief gave them one last grunt before waddling over to the door of Scarlett's apartment and holding court with the officers who were on the scene.

"That man is a waste of space," Hudson said.

Striker snorted. "I'd love to disagree with you, but I think you nailed it in one." He turned to Rhys. "Still, even a stopped clock is right twice a day. While I don't believe in coincidences enough to buy this isn't connected to the murder, the chief isn't wrong. Ms.

Jones wasn't working there when Windemere disappeared. What she and the doctor have in common is beyond me at this moment, but you can be certain I'll be looking into it."

"So do you want to talk to Scarlett?" Hudson asked.

Unease immediately rose in Rhys's gut. He did not want Scarlett talking to the cops, at least not without a lawyer present. He'd seen what those cops had done to Sunny. He didn't think Striker was an asshole like Chief Wells, but he wasn't comfortable taking the chance either.

"Easy son." Striker reached out and tapped Rhys's arm. "I don't need to speak with her tonight, but maybe we can have a chat tomorrow, at her convenience. I just want to nail down some details. She's not in any trouble."

Rhys nodded. He was pissed Striker could read him so easily...and baffled by his own reaction to Scarlett. Why was he so protective of someone he'd met only yesterday? She just touched off something in him. Maybe she reminded him of his sisters, and that was what was making him such a watchdog. He glanced at the truck. Her face was still pale, but it not as devoid of color as it had been earlier. Still, her big green eyes looked tired and scared. All he wanted to do was wrap her up in his arms and hold her. And he was honest enough to admit that had nothing to do with brotherly affection.

CHAPTER 7

"You okay?" Rhys's voice was soft and hard to make out over the sound of the truck's tires on the pavement.

"Yes." Scarlett turned her head and stared out into the darkness. She couldn't face him. The humiliation of almost passing out when she saw the mess in her apartment was too fresh in her mind. Trashed didn't begin to describe it. Nothing had escaped the intruder's wrath. Not one thing.

She'd been so sure she was ready to see it. That she could cope. But the moment she walked across the threshold, she'd been assaulted by the memory of her mother's body lying broken at the foot of the stairs, head surrounded by a pool of blood.

A soft curse escaped her lips, and she linked her fingers together to stop them from shaking.

"Sunny is making up one of the rooms at the

ranch. We'll all sleep there tonight. We can deal with...everything in the morning."

A wave of nausea overtook her. She did not want to see Hudson or Sunny right now. She couldn't bear to see their pitying looks or hear the sympathy in their voices. She couldn't bear to see the evidence of her own weakness. No. She wasn't weak. She was traumatized. That was what her therapist in L.A. had kept reminding her.

Heat crawled across her cheeks as bile rose in her throat. She opened the window a crack to get a blast of cold air on her face. "I... Can we not stay there? I just...can't..." She couldn't stop her voice from cracking.

She shot Rhys a quick glance. He caught her eye, and something shifted in his expression. She was pretty sure he'd been about to argue with her, but one look at her face had changed his mind.

"Sure. Ah, we can find a hotel in town...I guess." He started to slow the truck down so they could turn around.

"No. No hotel." The thought of other people being close by, of hearing their doors slam and their conversations as they went by...it was too much. She just wanted to feel safe and secure by herself. For whatever reason, Rhys was the only one she could tolerate right now. She licked her lips. "Can we just go to the cabin?"

"Ah, sure. I guess. If that's what you want. I don't think there's any food or anything like that."

"That's fine. I couldn't eat right now anyway."

Rhys frowned but remained silent. He pulled his phone out of his pocket and made a call.

Ten minutes later, they pulled up in front of the Riggs' ranch house.

"I thought we were staying in the cabin?" she blurted out.

"We are," he said in a hushed voice. "I just need to grab a few things. You want to stay in the truck? I won't be more than a couple of minutes."

He hopped out of the truck and took the steps two at a time. When he disappeared inside, a small cry escaped Scarlett's lips. Her whole body shook, and she rocked back and forth for a minute, trying to get herself under control again.

This was different. This wasn't about Scarlett, not really. Someone had a beef with the spa, and they'd chosen her as a target. None of this was personal. She tried to practice her yoga breathing. In. Out. In. Out. And it worked, mostly, but even though Rhys had left the truck running, the chill was starting to seep into her bones, and it was so much deeper and harsher than the chill of winter.

Rhys emerged from the ranch house carrying what looked like a huge picnic hamper. Huck, Hudson's mom's dog, was at his heels. Scarlett watched as Rhys put the hamper and a backpack in the back of the pickup. That done, he opened the driver's side door. Huck jumped in, tail already wagging furiously, and plopped himself down, right next to Scarlett.

"Hi, Huck," she murmured as she rubbed the fur behind his ears.

Rhys climbed in behind the wheel. "I thought Huck might like to join us tonight. That okay with you?"

"Sure," Scarlett murmured. She'd spent plenty of time with Huck while working on the ranch house. He'd kept her company on her many treks around the property when she was overseeing the redecoration of the outbuildings and the fences along the driveway of the ranch. As Rhys drove toward the cabin, the dog leaned into her, seeming to sense she needed a doggie hug. His warmth seeped into her, helping to ease some of the cold.

Five minutes later, Rhys parked the truck, and they all go out. Huck ran for the cabin door and looked back at them from the porch, tail wagging, waiting impatiently for them to let him in. Scarlett didn't blame him one bit. It was freezing. No, below freezing. The snow crunched under her boots, and her breath crystalized in the air in front of her.

Rhys grabbed the hamper and shot up the steps to open the front door. He took a brief look inside and then ushered Scarlett in. He came in behind her and set the hamper down on the counter and turned toward her. "I'll grab your bag. Why don't you take a seat on the sofa? I'll make a fire and get us something warm to drink in a minute."

Her bag. He meant the bag a police officer had packed for her since her apartment was a crime scene. She tried to take a deep breath, but it got caught in her throat.

She watched Huck run around and sniff everything for a second, but she didn't feel like sitting idle. So she took off her coat and hung it on the wall pegs by the door and then moved over to the fireplace and started building a fire.

She and her mom had owned a cabin in the mountains in California when Scarlett had been in high school. They'd always enjoyed going there for the holidays. Scarlett used to be in charge of the fire. Her mom was great at cooking and baking but utterly useless at building a proper fire. They'd sold that cabin when her mom had found Canyon Springs. Her mom had always intended to buy a place here but had never gotten around to it.

By the time Rhys was finished moving around behind her, Scarlett had the fire burning brightly. She turned to find him watching her. "Um, sorry. I thought it would be better if I just got it going. It's freezing out there."

"That's great. It gave me a chance to turn up the heat and get the water boiling for tea."

"I won't say no to a cup of tea. Thanks."

"Why don't you get yourself situated. I put your bag on the bed."

Scarlett frowned. When she made the request to stay here, she hadn't thought about the sleeping arrangements. There was only one bedroom, one bed. "Oh, God, I didn't mean to kick you out of your room." Her shoulders sagged.

"It's not a big deal. The couch pulls out, remember? I'll be absolutely fine out here. Nice and toasty next to the fire."

Scarlett opened her mouth to protest but shut it again. Who was she kidding? She wouldn't be able to sleep out here by herself, and there was no way Rhys would let her. "Um, if you're sure it's okay..."

"Yep, no worries. Go freshen up. The tea will be ready by the time you're finished. How do you take it?"

"Just a bit of milk."

"Okay," Rhys said as he puttered around the kitchen area. Scarlett walked across the floor into the bedroom. The brightly colored duvet cover greeted her, the bold color boosting her spirits.

She sat down on the bed and pulled off her boots. She should have taken them off by the door, but she'd forgotten. At least she hadn't tracked snow all over the place. It was one advantage of the spike heel; snow didn't stick to it.

As soon as she put her feet on the floor, she realized three things: one, her feet had been numb in her boots and now they hurt, two, the thin little socks she'd brought with her from California were not going to cut it during a Montana winter and three, the floor was cold. Good thing she'd put the throw rugs around. She made a mental note to get another large rug for the bedroom. The small one by the foot of the bed was not enough.

She opened the bag the policewoman had packed for her. The woman had obviously done this before. She'd grabbed all the right kinds of comfy clothing. After changing into a sleep shirt, yoga pants, and an oversize forest green sweater, Scarlett paused and then added a pair of socks before she made her way to the bathroom.

Once inside, she turned on the light and locked the second door leading to the main room. It was then she saw her reflection in the mirror.

Jesus, no wonder Rhys hadn't argued with her. Her cheeks were the color of paper, and her eyes had massive dark circles under them. She looked like hell. Her hair, which had been tied up, was sticking out in all directions. There was no point in being mortified about it now. She'd looked like this for hours. Rhys would just have to deal with it.

Scarlett washed her face and took her hair down before leaving the bathroom. Rhys had kept the lamps on but had turned off the harsher overhead light. He'd also turned on the Christmas tree lights.

He even had Christmas music playing quietly in the background.

"Your tea is on the coffee table," Rhys said. He was squatting down, putting something under the counter. When he came up, he froze for a second.

"Sorry. I know. I look like death warmed over."

"Uh, no. You look...that is, don't worry about it. You've been through a lot."

She frowned. What was that supposed to mean? He wasn't supposed to *agree* with her.

"Let me rephrase," he hurried on. "You look a little shell-shocked, and that's to be expected, but by no means do you look like hell." He smiled. "I like your hair down."

"Thanks." Scarlett smiled slightly as she headed over to the sofa and sat in front of the roaring fire. Maybe it was stupid of her to care about what Rhys thought of her appearance at this exact moment—or ever—but she did. He came over and sat on the other end of the sofa, which Huck apparently took as an invitation because he jumped up and curled into a ball between them.

Scarlett laughed and stroked Huck's fur. "Are you comfy?" He licked her hand in response.

It leached more of her tension away, and she shifted her attention to Rhys. "I want to apologize for how I reacted to seeing the apartment earlier. I guess I didn't realize how much all of this was affecting me."

His brows shot up. "Why would you need to apologize? That kind of destruction would be traumatizing for anyone, plus you've been carrying the load of this by yourself for weeks. Your reaction was perfectly normal."

She reached for the mug he'd prepared and took a sip of tea. It was perfect—just the way she liked it, strong with a splash of milk. "I wouldn't go that far. Normally, I can handle anything. I still can't believe I almost passed out." Her cheeks burned, and she couldn't meet his gaze.

"I've seen grown men hit the floor after seeing their stuff trashed by a home invader...and the level of destruction wasn't half as bad."

Scarlett closed her eyes. She'd blocked out the amount of damage, but the images weren't far from her subconscious. Thinking about it made her slightly queasy again. When Rhys swore, she opened her eyes.

He reached out and put a hand on Huck's head. Was it foolish of her to wish it had landed on her thigh instead? "I'm sorry, Scarlett. I didn't mean to remind you."

"No. Please. Don't apologize. It's fine. It's a huge mess, and I will deal with it," she said with a lot more resolve than she was feeling. She took another sip of tea. "In truth, it never really felt like home. I rented that apartment because I needed a place and it was available, not because I loved it. Maybe this is my chance to find a place I really like."

"That sounds like a great idea."

Scarlett glanced at Rhys. She still felt like an idiot for her behavior back at the apartment. She also knew in her heart that with all of the memories of her mom surfacing, she needed to talk about what happened. "Rhys, there's something I should probably tell you. It will help explain my behavior."

"Scarlett," he said, meeting her gaze. His soft gray eyes welled with sympathy. "It's been in the back of my mind since I met you that you looked familiar somehow. I finally put it together a couple of days ago. My sisters were big fans of *Cooking with Corinne*. I know what happened. You don't have to talk about it if you don't want to."

"No, it's about time I did." She gave him a small smile. "If you're okay with listening." He put his hand on her thigh and squeezed slightly, and because she liked the feel of it there, she layered her hand over it.

"When Mom landed the show, we had no idea how big it would be. She just shone in front of the camera. She was a natural, and she made people feel at home. Her career took off, but she didn't stop paying attention to me or anything. I never doubted I was priority one."

"Then everything changed. She started getting these notes from a stranger. She felt like she was being watched. She tried to get the police to help, but they said their hands were tied. They advised her to beef up her security, which she did, but he still found ways to torture her. He sent emails with pictures of her he'd taken the week before. It got so bad she didn't want to leave the house.

God, this next part... Scarlett's belly clenched. She paused and hauled in a deep, bolstering breath. "One night I went out to get some groceries. I thought it might inspire her if I picked up some of her favorite ingredients. Cooking had always been her go-to thing, but she wasn't interested at all anymore.

"When I got back to the house and opened the front door, I found the whole house had been trashed. Everything had been broken and torn apart. The cushions slashed, the drapes pulled down. Nothing had escaped his wrath. And my mother was lying all bent and broken at the bottom of the stairs. There was a pool of blood around her head. She was wearing her favorite nightgown..."

"Scarlett, I'm so very sorry." Rhys moved his arm around her shoulders and tried to hugged her close to him but Huck was in the way. She didn't care. She relished the feeling of safety having Huck and Rhys next to her provided.

"So when I saw my place with everything looking just like my mom's had that night, it was all just too much. Anyway, I wanted you to know because it might take me a bit to get back to normal, whatever that means. The trauma of it is obviously still with me."

"You don't have to explain trauma to me," Rhys said as he absently rubbed his leg.

"Oh, right. Sorry, Rhys."

"You don't have to apologize either. Did they ever get the guy?"

"No, my mother's murderer walks free. They know who it is, but there's no proof."

Rhys leaned over and kissed her forehead. "I am so very sorry Scarlett."

She gave him a tight smile. "So am I." A wave of fatigue washed over her. The warm fire, her early wakeup, and all the day's happenings had finally caught up to her. She needed sleep. "I'm sorry. I'm going to have to go to bed."

"Hey, no worries. You've had a hell of a day."

When Scarlett stood, Rhys followed suit. "Why don't you take Huck with you? He's not supposed to sleep on the beds, but he does it all the time. He's a great foot warmer." As if he understood, Huck jumped off the sofa in a flash and jogged toward the bedroom.

Scarlett laughed. "I guess he's decided for me." She smiled at Rhys. "Thanks again. For everything." She moved two steps closer, went up on tiptoes, and kissed him on the cheek. She stumbled as she was going back down, and Rhys caught her. Their gazes locked, and a thrill of electricity danced across her skin. She was fragile right now, and as much as she would enjoy falling for Rhys, she knew in her bones that this man could be her undoing.

"Um, well, good night," she said as she slowly backed away.

Rhys dropped his hands from her arms. "Good night. Scarlett. Sleep well."

But it took her a long time to go to sleep, and for once it wasn't because she was thinking about her mother, or whoever had been terrorizing her. She was thinking about Rhys. The fire of his skin. The heat in his eyes. And the way he made her wish for something more.

～

Scarlett sat bolt upright in bed, her heart pounding in her ears, her lungs on fire. He was here. In the house. He was here trying to kill her, too!

"Scarlett!"

Someone was holding her. She tried to fight them off, but they refused to let go.

"Scarlett!"

The voice was familiar, but she couldn't shake off the feeling of blind panic. She flailed about. Then a dog barked. Her mother didn't have a dog, so Scarlett finally opened her eyes and looked wildly around the room. She wasn't back in L.A. at her mom's house. She was in Canyon Springs. She blinked. Huck was beside her. He licked her cheek, his doggy face full of worry.

"Scarlett," the voice said.

She turned and realized it was Rhys. He was sitting on the edge of the bed, naked from the waist up. His brows were drawn together, and lines were etched around his mouth. His hands still gripped her forearms, his hold gentle but firm.

"Rhys, I... What's going on?"

"You were having a nightmare." He studied her closely. "Are you okay?"

She pushed her hair behind her ear with a shaky hand. "Yes." Which wasn't exactly true, but at least her heart rate was coming back to normal. The dream had been so vivid. She shuddered.

"I'll go make you some tea." He let go of her and started to get up.

Panic gripped her belly again. "Please don't go," she said. "I...I just need a minute or two." She couldn't meet his gaze.

He sat back down on the edge of the bed. "No problem."

She shot him a quick glance, although this time her eyes zeroed in on his chest. The muscles rippled as he created a more comfortable perch on the edge of the bed. His abs were shredded, and she had the desire to reach out and touch them.

"Do you want to talk about it?"

"What?" Her gaze shot up to meet his as heat bloomed across her cheeks.

"Your nightmare," Rhys said in a quiet voice. "Sometimes talking about them helps banish them."

"No. We talked about it earlier. I'd rather work on forgetting now." She turned away from his chest and glanced at Huck. He still looked so concerned. "Sorry, Huck. I didn't mean to scare you." She scratched him behind the ear. Huck pushed into her hand.

Rhys reached out and patted the dog's head. "You're okay, aren't you, Huck?" Huck licked his hand and then bent down for a good stretch, after which he shook himself. Then he stood, turned himself in a circle, and collapsed back down onto the bed. Within seconds, it seemed like he was asleep again.

Scarlett fervently wished she could go to sleep like that, but it wasn't going to happen for tonight or for a few nights to come.

"Scarlett," Rhys put his knuckle under her chin and forced her to meet his gaze. "Are you sure you don't want to talk about your mom some more?"

She swallowed the lump in her throat. She knew she could talk about her mom's murder until she was blue in the face, but it wouldn't change things. She needed time. Time to heal. Nothing else would work, but being held would help.

Needing to touch him, she threw her arms around his neck. Rhys's arms closed around her and brought her close, and she drank in his woodsy scent. She liked the feeling of their bodies pressed together far more than was wise. Logically, she knew he was the last person she should fall for. He was leaving. The smart thing to do would be to untangle herself and tell him goodnight, but she didn't want to be alone. The hell with being fragile. She wanted company—*his* company.

Rhys dropped his arms and drew back. "Scarlett—"

She swooped in and pressed her mouth to his. He stilled, his lips softer than she'd imagined. She nibbled on his bottom lip. Then she fisted his hair with one hand while she ran the other down his back, pulling him closer yet.

Rhys pulled away and held her at arms' length. "Fuck, Scarlett," he growled. Then he pulled her into his lap, crushed his mouth over hers, and kissed her with an urgency she felt to her toes.

CHAPTER 8

Rʜʏs ʜᴀᴅ ʙᴇᴇɴ ᴅʀᴇᴀᴍɪɴɢ about this since the first moment he'd seen her. She tasted like heaven, and their tongues danced with a fiery passion that had him desperate for more. He brought his hand up to cup her breast through her T-shirt. It was full, and he liked the weight of it in his palm. He rubbed back and forth over the nipple with his thumb. Scarlett moaned.

Rhys shifted her so she was directly on top of his crotch. Her heat seeped through his jeans, making him hard as rock. God, how he wanted to be inside her. He kissed the hollow of her neck and she whispered his name. He loved the way it sounded on her lips.

Rhys captured her mouth again and tangled his fingers into her hair. She started rocking back and forth on his crotch. Under her t-shirt he ran his hand up her belly and cupped her naked breast.

He had raised her T-shirt and brought his head down to suck her nipple when he heard Huck give a low warning growl deep in his throat.

Rhys immediately pulled back and looked at the dog. The fur was standing straight up along Huck's back.

"What? Why'd you stop?" When Scarlett followed Rhys's gaze to Huck, all the color left her face.

"Stay here with the dog," Rhys said as he got up and made for the door. He dropped low and did a fast glance down the hall and then a second sweep of the main room of the cabin. It was empty, but Huck was still growling softly on the bed. Rhys moved quickly through the darkness, keeping low until he reached the large picture window that overlooked the front yard and the valley below.

He did a quick check but saw nothing. He repositioned himself so he was leaning against the wall. It was dark out, but there was a crescent moon, its scant light reflected by the snow covering the ground. The cabin itself was dark. He hadn't stopped to hit the lights in the main room after Scarlett's scream awakened him.

He waited. He relaxed his breathing and stayed very still. Someone was out there. He knew it in his gut and the relief of knowing nearly staggered him. He searched the tree line on the left side of the cabin. It was the most likely place for someone to hide.

There! A figure was crouched on the far left, close to the fence, just before the ground fell away. Whoever it was had on dark colors. Coat, hat, gloves, even dark boots. He'd just caught sight of them framed against the sky before they disappeared into the trees.

He waited. The figure emerged again from the trees, turning toward the house. It had no face. Rhys's brain tried to make sense of what he was seeing. How could it have no face? There had to be a face. Was he losing it? Was his brain playing tricks on him?

Balaclava. Scarlett had said the intruder wore a black balaclava. Rhys was just too far away to discern the features. With that on at this distance, he wouldn't even see their eyes. He was tempted to run outside, but was only half dressed and the temp had to be in the single digits. He'd be frozen to the core before he got far.

He watched the faceless figure blend back into the tree line. After a couple minutes, Rhys knew the figure was gone. From now on, he would make sure there was a posted guard every night. Someone wanted something, and they thought Scarlett had it. Rhys was pretty sure he knew what it was.

He walked back into the bedroom. Scarlett was sitting up against the headboard with the blankets pulled up around her, her arms wrapped tightly around Huck. Her eyes were round, and her hands were shaking.

"Shit. Scarlett, everything is fine. You're safe." He came back over and sat down on the bed. Scarlett immediately let go of Huck and threw herself on his lap.

Fuck. He hadn't meant for her to be so scared. "Scarlett, shh, honey," he said as he stroked her back. "It's okay. You're safe."

"Are you sure? Was someone out there?" Her big green eyes were bright with unshed tears, and her lips were trembling.

His first instinct was to tell her the truth because he hated lies, but if he did, she would never get any sleep. "I think it was an animal of some kind. I didn't see it clearly." Which was technically true, in the sense that humans were animals and he *hadn't* seen the figure clearly.

He brushed the hair out of her eyes. He wanted desperately to pick up where they'd left off, but it would be a mistake. Scarlett was in a vulnerable position. The last thing he should do was take advantage of her, not to mention he felt like shit for having been so wrapped up in her he'd missed the intruder. It was like the incident in the Middle East all over again. His instincts worked fine...as long as he didn't get distracted. He pushed gently back on the bed and stood up.

"Where are you going?" Scarlett asked.

"You've been running yourself ragged on this job, and with everything else, I think maybe it's best if you try and rest. Huck will be here to keep you safe and warm."

Scarlett's eyes narrowed and then she frowned. Color rose in her cheeks. "Yes"—her voice sounded rough—"you're right. I could use some sleep." She shifted so she was back under the duvet, which she pulled up to her chin. "Thank you for checking things out for me. I appreciate it."

She wouldn't meet his gaze. He silently cursed his clumsiness. He wanted to make her understand that he didn't want to leave. He just needed to. Because if he didn't put some distance between them, he'd lose his perspective. He'd lose his ability to protect her. Even now, he could still feel her curves crushed against his chest. He cleared his throat. "Good night, Scarlett."

"Night, Rhys." It was hard to hear her because she had the duvet half covering her face. Huck glanced at Rhys and then back at Scarlett. He curled into a circle again and lay down on the bed next to Scarlett. *Good move, Huck. One of us should get to curl up next to her tonight.*

~

RHYS AWOKE to the sound of clanging pots. His eyes popped open, but he immediately closed them again.

The sunlight off the snow was making the room very bright. His body was very stiff and tired. Last night, he'd gone back to the couch and laid down, but sleep hadn't come easily. The sofa bed wasn't all that comfortable, and he was worried.

He'd eventually texted Hudson an explanation of what had happened, and Hudson had promised to send some guys over immediately to keep an eye on the place. Rhys hadn't relaxed until he'd received the text that said they'd arrived. By then, it had been almost dawn.

He glanced at his watch. It was still early. The pots clanked again. He cursed silently and slowly got off the sofa bed. "Morning, Scarlett."

"Good morning, Rhys." Her smile was tight and her movements jerky. *Shit*. She was pissed with him. He'd spent enough time around his sisters to know what a woman's silent anger looked like. Unfortunately, she was going to have to stay angry.

He'd had plenty of time to think about his actions while lying on the sofa bed waiting for the Brotherhood guys to show up. He'd acted irresponsibly toward his client. Okay, she wasn't a paying client, but he'd accepted responsibility for her. He couldn't make out with her, no matter how alluring she was. It broke all the rules. He needed to maintain distance and objectivity and, most importantly, he needed to be able to focus. Because he knew firsthand, bad things happen when he got distracted on a job.

He went into the bedroom, grabbed some clothes, and then took a shower. Toweling himself off afterward, he glanced at his scar. The shot had been a through and through so he had a corresponding scar on the back of his thigh. They were both still red and puckered, but at least they didn't hurt anymore.

The doc at the spa had helped him enormously with that. He was grateful. He'd worried he might be done in the personal protection field. Who wants a guy who can't run? But she'd worked her medical magic for him, and he was back in business. At least physically. His instincts were fine, too. If he could just keep himself focused, he'd be golden.

He got dressed and headed out into the main room. Scarlett was loading the dishwasher. She'd gone through the rations he'd stolen from the ranch house last night and made herself breakfast. Eggs if he had to guess. She hadn't left any for him. Looked like he'd have to get some food on the road. He walked over and grabbed himself a mug and went to the coffee pot. At least she'd left him some, even if it was slightly cool. Much like her attitude toward him.

"So, what do you have on for today?" he asked as he put his coffee in the microwave. He hated cold coffee.

Scarlett continued to flit around the space, cleaning and straightening everything in sight. "All of the furniture is being delivered this week. I need to be there to see that it's properly installed. The medical equipment is already in place, but more beds, chairs, and desks are coming. They're also installing the desk in reception and finishing the waterfall."

Scarlett brushed past him, and her scent engulfed him. It made him think about how well she'd fit in his lap last night. He grabbed his coffee out of the microwave and took a large sip.

"Fuck!" he slammed the mug down on the counter. The too-hot liquid had burned the inside of his mouth.

Scarlett stopped wiping the table and raised an eyebrow at him. "Problem? Something too hot for you to handle?"

Rhys froze with his coffee cup halfway to his mouth again. His gaze locked with Scarlett's, and her cheeks turned that now familiar shade of pink. It matched her current sweater.

According to his sisters, not many redheads could get away with wearing pink, but Scarlett's pale cashmere sweater was perfect. He was pretty sure it was cashmere, again, thanks to his sisters. On the other hand, his sisters had nothing to do with him noticing how the sweater hugged Scarlett's curves.

Truthfully, it was hard for him not to notice Scarlett, no matter what she was wearing. He admired her ass as she leaned over to finish wiping the table. Her jeans hugged it just right. He was willing to bet it would fit perfectly in his hands. He hadn't had the chance to check last night but it sure as hell fit perfectly in his lap.

He cursed silently. Scarlett was way too distracting.

"Look, Hudson and Sunny are going to take you into the spa today. I'll meet you there later."

She walked back over to the kitchen area and put the sponge in the sink. "Why is that? I thought you were in charge of keeping me safe."

"I am, but I have a couple of things to take care of today."

Her eyes narrowed.

He quickly made a decision. "Scarlett, I lied to you. Not because I wanted to, but because I knew you wouldn't get any rest if I told you the truth. There was someone outside last night."

"Sonuvabitch. Why didn't—? Forget it. I get it." She leaned against the opposite counter, her shoulders slumping.

He was pretty sure he saw tears in her eyes, but she wouldn't meet his gaze. For once, he was glad. If she did, he'd be forced to hug her, and if he had her in his arms...

Well, he wouldn't be able to stop himself after that. He was trying to be reasonable and not take advantage of her, but she'd shown him last night she was game.

Or maybe you're just being a coward.

Scarlett was the type of woman men fell head

over heels for. He just couldn't afford to risk it. He *was* leaving after Christmas. Being over there with his head and heart over here would be a death sentence.

"What things do you have to take care of today?" she asked finally.

"I'm meeting with a group of guys from the Brotherhood Protectors. They're going to be outside from now on. As a matter of fact, some of them arrived last night. I texted Hudson after you went back to sleep, and he sent some guys over. I made sure they were in place before I got some shuteye."

He took a sip of coffee. His mouth hurt. "Scarlett, I need you to understand this is escalating. The person who's after you has proven they're willing to take bigger risks. That makes them dangerous. You won't be alone from now on until this is over."

Scarlett's eyes got shiny again, but she just nodded. "I understand." But barely a beat passed before she said more emphatically, "No. I don't understand. What is it they're after?"

He'd given that plenty of thought, too, the night before.

"I think I've got a pretty good idea."

A knock sounded at the door at the same time Rhys's phone pinged. He glanced at the screen—Hudson—before heading to the door and opening it.

"Hey, Rhys. Hey, Scarlett. You ready to go?"

"Just give me a minute." Scarlett bustled into the bedroom and closed the door.

"How are you doing? You look like shit." Hudson hit Rhys in the gut on his way to the coffee pot.

"Coffee's cold." Rhys said. "And I'm doing fine other than missing sleep. Are the new guys here?"

"Be here in about thirty minutes. Griffin Kane will be your point of contact. He pulled together the team that arrived earlier. He'll organize the rest of guys in shifts and take it from there. I've given you the friends and family discount but it's still going to cost you. The guys have to get paid."

"I'm happy to pay full price if necessary. I don't want Scarlett to be left unprotected and I know the guys deserve every cent."

There was a knock at the door, and Hudson cocked his head. "You expecting anyone else?"

"No." Rhys walked over and opened the door. "Striker. Come on in."

Bill Striker entered the cabin and wiped his boots on the rug. "Hey, Rhys. Hudson, glad you're here too. Saves me trying to find you."

"What brings you by?" Rhys's heart thumped in his chest. He prayed there wasn't more bad news for Scarlett.

"I have some new information on the situation, and I want your take on it."

Hudson's eyebrows went up. "Okay. You want

coffee?" He gestured toward the pot. "Rhys here will make it for you."

Rhys laughed. "Sure, I'll make a pot."

"Don't bother on my account," Striker said. "I've already had too many cups this morning."

Rhys gestured toward the table. "Why don't we all sit."

Striker took off his jacket and put it over the back of his chair as the men grabbed seats around the dining table. "Where's Scarlett? June, from the diner, mentioned that Sunny's grandmother Clara, told her Scarlett's staying here with you, Rhys."

Rhys shook his head. "This small town's gossip network is unbelievable. Scarlett's getting ready to go to work."

Striker nodded. "So, we have some time then."

Rhys said, "Yup. So what's up?"

"Well, after talking with Sunny yesterday, I did a bit of digging. Turns out Scarlett is not the only one to experience a break-in."

"Huh." Hudson took another sip of coffee. "What are you thinking, Striker?"

Rhys cut him off. "Let me take a guess. You're thinking that whoever murdered Skip Windemere didn't find the money and they're out there searching for it. At least that's my theory."

Striker gave a curt nod. "It does explain things. They probably think it's at the Wellness Retreat. Or, at least, they did in the beginning. It explains why they stole the keys and those blueprints."

Hudson nodded. "Makes sense, I guess, but how come we didn't hear anything about other break-ins?"

Striker growled, "Chief Wells was keeping a tight lid on the situation because he doesn't want people to panic. Or so he claims. It's why he didn't bother to share the information, even after he heard about us finding the doctor's body. 'Probably kids,' is his official response."

Rhys snorted. "Kids are responsible for all the crime in Canyon Springs according to him. But here's the thing. Why Scarlett? Why not break into Sunny's place? Wouldn't she be the logical choice, or the general contractor?"

Striker frowned and looked down. "Well, I haven't exactly been forthcoming myself on that score." He drummed his fingers on the table. "Someone broke into Miss Clara's place a couple of weeks ago. On the timeline, it was probably one of the first break-ins."

"Why am I just finding out about this now?" Hudson demanded.

"You know Clara. She hates Wells after what happened with Sunny. She called me, but swore me to secrecy. I sent a couple of deputies around, but Clara said nothing was missing and the damage was minimal. Clara had left the window open a crack, and the intruder came in that way.

"I know Sunny's going to be mad when she hears this, but tell her not to panic too much. Clara is fine, and I've been asking a couple of my guys to take a run by Clara's a couple times during the night to make sure she's okay. It's not my jurisdiction, but their doing it as a personal favor to me.

Clara and I go way back. She took care of my mom all those years ago when she was in hospice care at the hospital and Clara was still a nurse. I've never forgotten how she went out of her way for me and my dad."

Hudson nodded. "I appreciate that, Striker, but it wouldn't have been necessary if you'd just said something."

"I have lived a long life by knowing when to open my mouth and when to keep a secret. If Miss Clara says don't tell, I won't tell. I have no desire to be on that woman's bad side."

Hudson grinned. "I hear what you're saying. She's a bit of a handful."

Striker leaned back in his chair. "The reality is the break-in happened during the day anyway. I didn't think it was likely to happen again, and now with the everything that's come to light, I'm inclined to think it's safe. The killer has crossed Sunny off the list."

Rhys played with his coffee mug. "So you think the killer is systematically searching for the money"

Striker nodded. "I do."

Rhys cocked his head. "But, surely, not everyone

has had a break-in. Chief Wells couldn't keep all of those break-ins a secret. Not in a town this size."

"No, you're right. Not everyone who's been working on the project or had access to the Wellness Retreat has had a break-in, but I have a theory about that. I think we're looking for a local."

"A local? Why?" Hudson asked.

"Because if you look at the list of people who would have access and compare it to those who haven't had a break-in, something becomes abundantly clear."

Hudson put his mug down on the table. "What?"

Striker pulled out two pieces of paper from his jacket pocket. "You tell me."

Hudson took the papers and started perusing them. Rhys joined him by looking over his shoulder.

Hudson grinned. "I see what you're saying."

Rhys frowned. "I don't."

"You wouldn't," Hudson said. "You have to know the locals to see it."

Striker nodded. "Rhys, all the guys that have worked on the spa project and haven't had their places searched are, well, not the swiftest bunnies in the woods. They're the type if they found that kind of money, they'd yell it from the rooftops. Or go down to their favorite bar and buy everyone a round or two. They wouldn't be able to keep silent about it. Not for a minute."

Rhys nodded. "So, whoever the killer is has to have that same local knowledge."

"Yes, a local makes the most sense," Striker agreed.

Rhys frowned. "But why did the killer trash Scarlett's place so badly, assuming it was the killer?"

Striker took the pieces of paper back from Hudson. "I think the killer is getting frustrated and might be panicking."

Rhys's gut knotted. Striker's words echoed his fears. A frantic killer meant things could go downhill fast.

Striker put his elbows on the table. "Rhys, that's why I came out here. We found the body yesterday and Scarlett's place was trashed last night. Whoever it is has to be worried now. I know the ranch is well protected, but if you need some extra manpower, I can see what I can do."

"Way ahead of you on that score," Rhys said. "There was an incident here last night. We didn't bother with calling Wells, but someone was watching the cabin. Huck growled and alerted us to it, but I didn't get a good look. Anyway, Hudson sent some guys from the Brotherhood Protectors out last night and there's a new group arriving this morning. As a matter of fact, they should be here any minute."

"I'm glad to hear it," Striker said while pushing his chair back from the table. "I've got to run. Please keep me informed of any developments, and I'll do the same when I can."

Rhys nodded.

Hudson spoke up. "Striker, thanks for sharing the intel. It's greatly appreciated and thanks for looking out for Clara."

Striker put on his jacket. "All part of the job." When he rounded the table, both Rhys and Hudson stood. They all shook hands, and then Striker walked to the door. "Give my best to Scarlett."

Rhys nodded. "Will do."

After Striker took his leave, Rhys looked at Hudson. "What do you think?"

"I think we're going to keep a close eye on everything and everyone. There's a killer out there who's getting desperate."

"Agreed." Tension climbed from Rhys's gut to rest between his shoulder blades. He had to be on his game no matter what from now on. Scarlett's life could depend on it.

Hudson looked around the cabin. "This turned out really nice by the way. Scarlett did an awesome job."

"Tell her that. She needs all the positive vibes she can get. This whole thing has thrown her for a loop." He rubbed between his eyes. Hudson glanced at his watch and then the bedroom door and raised an eyebrow.

Rhys shrugged. "It's always been a mystery to me what they do in there." He poured himself more coffee and put it in the microwave.

The bedroom door opened, and Scarlett came out. She already had her coat on. She'd put her hair up, but a few wisps had escaped and were curling around her face. She'd added a touch of makeup that made her green eyes look huge and put some color in her cheeks. If Rhys had to guess, she'd spent most of the time she was in there covering the dark circles under her eyes. She looked beautiful to him, with or without the circles.

"Ready to go?" Scarlett asked as she gathered her stuff.

Hudson nodded. "I'll check in with you later, Rhys. Let me know how it goes with Griffin."

"Will do. Scarlett, I'll see you in a couple of hours."

She gave him a tight smile, and then she was gone. Hudson nodded goodbye and closed the door. Rhys looked down at his reheated coffee and then poured it down the drain. His gut was churning. Everything in his body was telling him that they'd gotten lucky so far—but if he knew anything, it was that luck always ran out. Now that the pressure was on, the real nightmare was just beginning.

CHAPTER 9

SCARLETT WIPED the back of her neck with an old hand towel. It was cold inside the medical wing of the spa, but after spending the morning unpacking and moving furniture, she built up a sweat. She took a swig from her water bottle, watching as a couple of guys brought in a set of cabinets. "Don't put that on its side. It'll break." She got up and moved across the room. "Put it on its back."

The two movers stopped. One of them rolled his eyes, but they did as they were told. Scarlett bit her tongue. It was taking a lot longer than she'd hoped for all the furniture to be placed, and there'd already been some mix-ups. With Christmas only two days away, it was hard to get anyone to focus on work.

Herself included. She was tired and frustrated, too, but it all needed to get done. "Look, I know you're probably pretty tired at this point. We've been at this for three days. I feel exactly the same way. Why don't you go back out to the lobby and grab some cookies? I just refilled the plates."

The guys mumbled their thanks and hightailed it out of the room. Scarlett knelt and started peeling the packing off the cabinets. She winced. It had been three very long days of getting things organized. Her fingers had all kinds of nicks and cuts, and she was exhausted beyond belief. She and Rhys were still being cool to one another, and although having the other men around watching the place made her feel better, she still hadn't gotten much sleep.

"Hey, need some help in here?" She looked up and saw Sunny standing in the doorway.

"That's okay. I can manage."

"I know you can manage," Sunny said as she walked into the room. "You've been doing an amazing job. I can't tell you how many compliments I've received from people who've seen it. I took some of the docs and nurses through last night, and they can't wait to get back to work. They're super excited about their new space, and they're thrilled with the addition of the doctors and nurses' lounge. That was a fabulous idea. They're already calling this their home away from home."

Scarlett smiled. "I'm thrilled they're happy."

"You should be so proud of yourself. You've made a real difference already. The last small group tour just ended so I can take over and you can get out of here."

Scarlett felt her eyes go wide. "W-what?"

"Go home or back to the cabin. You've lived this project from the very beginning, and I appreciate it more than I can say. It just proves that I hired the right person for the job but, honestly, there isn't enough makeup on earth to cover those black circles under your eyes. You've arrived early and stayed late every night this week. We're going to open on time. Please. Just go and relax."

"But there's still so much to do." She stood up, her heart thumping faster in her chest. "There's still stuff to unwrap and set up, and there's the punch list to consider. I know the movers bumped the wall in exam room three. I need to go through the place and note every detail so the crew can come in and fix everything."

"Scarlett," Sunny said, her tone soft but firm. "This is no longer a suggestion. You're leaving now. It will all still be here tomorrow. I told Rhys you were leaving. He's waiting for you in the lobby."

Scarlett looked down at the cabinet and then back at Sunny. Now that she'd been given permission to feel it, a wave of exhaustion descended on her, weakening her knees. Work had been her solace. It had helped her forget, if only momentarily, that someone was after her. It had helped her forget that Rhys had rejected her. But forgetting something didn't make it go away.

"You know what, you're right," she admitted. "I'm bushed. This week has been a bit hard. Thanks for giving me a nudge. I'll be back tomorrow morning."

Sunny smiled. "Please, not before nine. Ten or eleven would be better."

"Okay, I won't make any promises about the time. There's still lots to do," she mumbled as she looked around the room.

"Enough!" Sunny threw Scarlett her coat and gathered her bags. "Do you need all this stuff at home?"

Scarlett looked down at the bags she always lugged around with her. "No. Not really. I won't be using anything tonight. It's my design notes and samples."

"Well, then those definitely stay here! No work tonight."

"Sunny—"

"Go!" she ordered in a voice that brooked no argument.

Scarlett nodded. "Thank you. See you tomorrow." She moved into the hallway as an ear-splitting alarm sounded. "What's that?" she yelled as Sunny entered the hallway.

"The emergency exit alarm. Someone must have tried to open the back door." Sunny started down the hallway toward the back of the building. Scarlett fell in step but texted Rhys to let him know she was fine and what was happening. She didn't want him to come running.

They rounded the corner and Scarlett walked directly into a woman. "Oh," she said as she jumped back. "Sorry, Megan, isn't it? I didn't see you there."

Sunny hustled over to the alarm panel next to the emergency exit door at the end of the hallway just as Donna came out of a room.

"What's that sound?" Donna yelled.

"The emergency exit alarm," Sunny yelled back. She punched in an alarm code and the sound stopped.

"Sorry about that. Did one of you ladies hit the door?" Sunny asked.

"Ah, no. We were in the bathroom after our tour and then we got kind of lost." Donna said.

"We didn't touch the door though, honest," Megan chirped. Her eyes were big and her cheeks were a bit pale.

Scarlett wondered what was really going on but Sunny just smiled at the two women. "Well I hope you enjoyed your tour. Why don't we walk you back to the main doors?" Sunny gestured toward the end of the hallway and the group started walking.

"You did a wonderful job on the Retreat center ladies." Donna said.

Sunny was quick to respond with a big smile. "Thank you. I am so pleased you like it."

Scarlett tried to muster up a real smile but she was dead on her feet suddenly and all she wanted to do was escape. "Thanks," she mumbled.

Scarlett was about to ask Sunny about her Christmas plans when she noticed Sunny's expression. Her eyes were slightly narrowed and her lips pursed. Did something happen on the tour? She thought about asking, but it really wasn't the time. Maybe later or tomorrow.

"Oh sorry. I didn't hear what you said." Scarlett frowned. She'd been lost in thought and missed the conversation. The other ladies were looking at her.

Meg smiled. "We were just saying how amazing everything looks. We can't wait to get back to work here, right Donna?"

"What? Oh, right, yes. Can't wait." Donna's smile was tight.

Scarlett noted she wasn't the only one who wasn't paying attention. "I'm so glad." They walked down the maze of hallways to the foyer.

Rhys was standing beside the new reception desk, waiting for her. She gave him a tight, tired smile. She still didn't quite know how to act around him. They'd never discussed what had happened between them the other night, and it hadn't been repeated, more's the pity.

"Have a nice evening, ladies," Scarlett said as she watched them walk out the door. Sunny stood at the doorway and studied the two women as they walked across the parking lot.

"Sunny, is there something up?" she asked.

"Um…" She looked at Scarlett and then shook her head. "No, it's all fine. You go on and get out of here. Have a good night. You too, Rhys." She turned and headed back the way they'd come.

"Night, Sunny," Scarlett called.

"You ready to go? Rhys asked.

"Yes."

"Scarlett," a voice called, and Andy came across the lobby. He rested the ladder he'd been carrying on the floor.

"Hi, Andy, all finished?"

"Yup. I'll come in between Christmas and New Years to do any touch-ups. Just send me a punch list and let me know what day works best for you."

Scarlett smiled. "Thanks so much. You and your crew did an amazing job."

"Thanks, but you designed it. We just slapped paint on the walls."

"You're being too modest. Really, you saved my bacon getting those red walls covered so quickly." She shivered at the memory.

Andy's face clouded. "I'm still stumped about that one. Not once, on any of my other jobs, has something like that happened."

"Well, I'm just grateful you took care of it so quickly."

"We aim to please." He smiled and started to hoist the ladder, but he stopped and turned back to her. "I almost forgot. Here." He pulled Montana Moose out of his pocket. "I think you should take him home so he can watch over your next job."

Scarlett laughed and took the stuffed animal. "Thank you so much. He is a good watch moose. You have a wonderful Christmas."

Andy picked up the ladder. "You, too, Scarlett." He nodded to Rhys and then left.

Scarlett fluffed up the moose's fur and then looked around for a second.

"What?" Rhys asked.

"I decided—or rather Sunny decided—I should leave my bags here tonight, so I don't have anywhere to tuck this little guy." She shrugged slightly and jammed him into her coat pocket. "Let's go."

They'd developed a system over the last few days. Rhys always went out first to check things, and then he would hustle Scarlett across the parking lot to the truck. She suspected that he had guys from the Brotherhood Protectors watching the spa while she was there, but she hadn't asked. Rhys had been keeping his distance, and so had she.

The humiliation was a hard pill to swallow. He'd kissed her like he was starving and then pushed her away. To be fair, she'd thrown herself at him, something she'd never done before. Did that mean she was the one who had to smooth things over? She rubbed her temples. She was giving herself a headache.

"You okay?" Rhys asked in a quiet voice.

"Yes. Just a bit of a headache." She looked out the window and realized they were coming up on the diner. "Can we stop and pick up some food? I love their burgers."

Rhys kept driving past the diner.

"Rhys?"

"I already have dinner. I picked it up before I got you. I got them to use the heat packs so it should still be warm when we get back."

She wasn't sure what to say to that, so she settled on a simple response. "Okay."

The rest of the drive back to the cabin passed in silence. Scarlett was lost in her thoughts. It was her first Christmas without her mother. She was glad she was so damn tired and busy, otherwise she'd be a total mess.

When Rhys pulled up to the cabin, Griffin materialized to open her door. She never saw where he came from or where he disappeared to. She was quite sure he had magical powers. He was the strong, silent type, and she found him intimidating as hell, but he was always courteous, and she had to admit it made her feel so much safer having him and Rhys around.

Well, them and Huck. He'd snuggled with her every night. If she got any sleep at all it was because of that old farm dog. She trusted his instincts. Huck had growled that first night to warn them about the intruder, so if he was snoring beside her, she knew it was okay to close her eyes.

Speaking of Huck...

"Where's Huck?" Scarlett asked as she walked through the door into the cabin. They usually picked him up on their way by the ranch house. Griffin had peeled off again, not following them inside.

"He decided to stay back at the ranch."

She cocked an eyebrow at Rhys.

"Seriously. I went to get him on my way into town, and he refused to get up. He was curled up on his pillow in front of the heater." Rhys took off his coat and hung it up. He put his gloves in his coat pockets and hat on the hooks by the door.

Scarlett frowned as she took off her hat and gloves. "Do you think he's okay? Maybe he ate something that upset his belly. Should we call the vet? Did you tell Hudson?"

"Huck is getting old. He probably just wanted to sleep in his own bed."

Scarlett blinked. "Oh." It was all she could think to say.

Rhys glanced over at her as he went to get plates. "Scarlett, you'll be fine here without him. I'm here, and Griffin and his boys are outside. You're safe. I promise."

"Right." Logically, she knew that, but she'd miss Huck. As she hung up her coat, her mind returned to his other comment. *He probably just wanted to sleep in his own bed.* Was that true of Rhys, too? He'd only slept in his bed once before she'd stolen it, and the sofa bed couldn't be that comfortable. She bit her lip. She needed to clean up her apartment and move back into it, but it had been infiltrated, and the thought of going back there sent tremors through her body.

"Why don't you go sit down?" Rhys said gently. "I'll bring the food over."

"Sure." Scarlett went over and sat down at the table. She would have normally left the curtains open so she could see the Christmas lights she'd made Rhys install on the front porch, but nothing about this situation was normal. The thought of someone being able to look in terrified her.

"Here you go." Rhys set the plate down in front of Scarlett. It was a cheeseburger deluxe platter from the diner. Just what she would have ordered.

"How did you know I've been dreaming about this all day?" She looked him in the eyes and held it for the first time in days.

Rhys smiled. "I just figured you deserved a treat after the week you've had." He gave her a wink and started eating his own cheeseburger.

She looked down at the meal in front of her and felt like a horrible human being. This man had been so good to her, and she'd been a cold bitch all week. It wasn't his fault he didn't want her. She frowned.

"Scarlett, are you okay?"

"Yes." She sighed. "It's just been a long week." She wanted to apologize, but if she did, she'd start sobbing. Her mother had always reminded her to take breaks. To stop what she was doing to eat and have a cup of tea. *You can't run on empty all the time and be successful.* She took a bite of her cheeseburger. It was heaven. "These burgers are magical."

Rhys laughed. "I think that's stretching it a bit far, but they sure are tasty."

They ate in a companionable silence until Scarlett couldn't make room for another bite. Rhys told her to take a seat on the couch while he cleaned up and made tea. Part of her felt inclined to argue—to insist on helping—but she didn't. She just sat down to admire the Christmas tree. It looked fabulous there in the corner with the lights twinkling. It made the cabin smell wonderful, too.

Tomorrow was Christmas Eve. She'd get up bright and early tomorrow and make some gingerbread cookies. That would add to the holiday scent in the cabin. She and her mother had baked every Christmas Eve for as long as she could remember.

Rhys sat down beside her and handed her a cup of tea. "What are you thinking about?"

Scarlett burrowed deeper into the cushions and rested her head against the back of the sofa. "My mom," she said in a quiet voice.

"Do you usually spend Christmas with your family?"

"It was just me and my mom, but we'd always spend it together. We would bake all morning on Christmas Eve day and then run around like crazy and deliver cookies to everyone all afternoon. We'd be exhausted by the time the day was over, so we would order Chinese food for dinner and spend the evening eating and watching our favorite movies."

Scarlett took a sip of her tea. "I thought I might do some baking tomorrow if that's okay."

Rhys grinned. "I love your cookies, so please bake as much as you'd like."

"Gingerbread and..." The lump in her throat suddenly got huge, and she couldn't speak. She took another sip of tea, hoping it would wash down the tears.

"Scarlett, are you okay?"

She nodded. "Tell me about your family."

Rhys sighed. "My old man walked out when I was small. Went for milk and never came back. Left my mom with the six of us to raise all on her own. She died a few years ago. Cancer. Now it's me and my five sisters, plus their various husbands and children."

"Won't you miss them since it's Christmas?"

Rhys was silent for a long moment. He stared at the tree. "Yes, I'll miss them. I miss them all the time, but they're really...overwhelming. It's kind of like having five mothers. As the youngest, I was always babied, and even though I'm a grown man, it's hard for them to see me that way.

"They also bring a lot of noise and chaos and upheaval. Sometimes it's too much for me, but I love seeing my nieces and nephews. There's nothing better than playing with them before bed. I get them all riled up and then hand them over to my sisters." A smile drifted across his face. "They complain, but I know they secretly love it just as much as I do. Still, they're all up in each other's business. They even live in the same neighborhood. I don't know how their husbands cope."

Scarlett found herself smiling, too. "I wish I had a big family. It was just me and Mom. My dad died when I was a baby. Heart attack. Mom and I did everything together. It was us against the world. We actually worked together before I started my interior design career." Her smiled faded. "I miss her so very much. Christmas won't be the same without her."

CHAPTER 10

"I WISH there was a way I could make it better, Scarlett," Rhys said. "Christmas can be a tough time of year."

She pulled away. "You've done so much for me already. You believed me when I didn't even believe myself, and you've kept me safe all week. I owe you for all of this."

He was torn. He wanted so desperately to pull her into his lap and kiss her. To show her this was so much more than a job for him. He *cared* about her. But he was still on duty until this guy was caught. And he was still leaving in a week or so. At least he thought he was leaving. He wasn't so sure he wanted to go anymore.

You don't have to, a voice inside of him argued. *Hudson wants you to stay.*

But he wasn't sure what to do about the other

voice, the one that kept telling him he had to prove he could still do the job. So he just said, "Let's call it even."

She let out a snort. "I haven't done a thing for you except bake cookies, so how can we be even? I could bake you cookies for the rest of your days, and we *still* wouldn't be even. Not even close."

Rhys scratched the stubble along his jaw. "You've helped me, too. I was having a hard time after I got shot." He reached forward and grabbed his mug of tea. Right now, he'd kill for a shot of bourbon. "I let myself get distracted on my last job overseas, and now I'll bear the mark of it for the rest of my life."

"Wait. Hudson said you got shot saving his life."

"Hudson exaggerates," he said, running a hand through his hair. "The job had gone to shit. He was pinned down, and I was giving him cover fire. A kid, he couldn't have been more than five or six, came out of a building a few doors down, and I hesitated. I let him distract me so I didn't see the other shooter on the roof. I got hit in the leg." He took a sip of now lukewarm tea. He leaned forward and put the cup back on the coffee table.

"I lost focus for just a second, and it could have gotten someone killed. I'm lucky it didn't." Scarlett rubbed his back. He loved her touch. It made his heart give a mighty thump in his chest every single time.

"You were worried about hurting an innocent

child, Rhys. That doesn't mean you're bad at your job. It just means you're a decent human being. I don't know much about what you do, but I think anyone would be shaken by what you saw. I wouldn't want to know someone who *wasn't* shaken by that."

"Still, it was a loss of concentration, and my training is supposed to help me stay laser-focused through everything. I was worried that I might have lost my edge, but I've realized something over the last week. My body is fine, and my instincts are as strong as ever. I know I can do my job and do it well. I feel it in my bones. I'm ready to get back to work." He turned to face her. "So that's the silver lining for me, I guess. It means a lot to me that you trusted me enough to protect you."

His readiness wasn't the only silver lining. This woman had awakened something in him. Desire flooded his system, and he saw his feelings mirrored in her eyes. He clamped his jaw shut. If he stayed close to her, he'd be kissing her within seconds. His phone rang, and he shot off the couch. Saved by the fucking bell.

"Beckett," he growled, answering.

"Rhys, it's Striker. Everything okay?"

"Striker. Yeah, fine. What's up?" Rhys walked over to the kitchen area and leaned against the counter.

"I thought you'd like to know there was an incident at the Wellness Retreat this evening. Someone tried to break in. We got him. His name is Dr. Nathan Kyle."

Rhys frowned. "A doctor? Why would he want to break in? Do you think it's him? Is he the killer?"

Scarlett got up and came over to stand next to Rhys.

Striker continued. "Dr. Kyle is in serious financial trouble. Apparently, he'd heard a rumor about his colleague being killed before he could get away with the money and it's still hidden at the spa. He figured he'd poke around. See if he could find it. That's all he's admitting to at the moment. I'll keep on it and take a closer look at his background."

"What's your gut say, Striker? Is he the one who's been harassing Scarlett?"

Scarlett's face lost some color, and Rhys reached out and squeezed her arm.

Striker hesitated. "I don't know… It seems to fit. He's desperate for money. So desperate that he risked breaking in. He lawyered up pretty quickly, but I'm going to go back in to take another crack at him. Shit. I've got to go. Chief Wells just arrived. He's going to want in on this. Damn good thing the spa, sorry Wellness Retreat, falls on my side of the line," Striker said. "I'll keep you updated."

"Thanks," Rhys said and clicked off the call.

"Well?" Scarlett asked.

Rhys explained the situation.

"Do you think it's him? This Dr. Kyle? Do you think he's the one who's been harassing me?"

"It's possible. Striker's going to take another shot at him and see if he can shake out any more information."

Scarlett rubbed her hands across her face. "It's got to be him. How many desperate people can there be in one town?"

"Probably more than we think, but I know what you mean. If the shoe fits..."

Scarlett looked up at Rhys. Her hair was down and curling around her shoulders. Her big green eyes gleamed at him, and her scent surrounded him. It was all too much. He could only be strong for so long, and maybe he didn't *need* to hold back anymore. If this guy was the one who'd broken into her house and frightened her, he was in police custody at the moment.

He reached for Scarlett, and she was in his arms in an instant. He claimed her mouth as he brought her full against him. She made a small moaning sound that had him rock hard in an instant, and he ran his hands down her back to cup her ass.

She fisted his hair as their tongues rolled and twisted in a fiery dance. The need to touch her, to feel her soft skin, consumed him, and he slid one hand up the back of her green sweater.

"Rhys," she whispered, arching into him as he kissed the hollow of her neck, "take your shirt off."

He reached back and grabbed a handful of his shirt, bringing it over his head in one swift movement before claiming her lips again in a scorching kiss. Then, because fair was fair, he put both hands under Scarlett's sweater and swiftly brought it up over her head. He dropped it to the floor and drank in the sight of her.

Her breasts were covered in a dark green lacy bra that matched her eyes. Rhys let out a groan. "You're gonna be the death of me." He took a moment to admire her, then reached around and undid her bra, letting the lacy confection drop to the kitchen counter. Her eyes had turned a brilliant green, and he watched them darken as he rubbed his thumbs across her nipples. He cupped her breast and sucked one nipple and then the other. Scarlett moaned and said his name.

"Say it again," he demanded. He loved the sound of his name on her lips.

She did, staring at him as she said it. He picked her up and carried her over to the soft leather sofa. He placed her gently on her back and then slowly lowered himself on top of her, dropping little kisses down her jawline. Alternating nipping and licking until he reached the hollow of her throat. She wound her fingers through his hair and opened her legs. After he lay directly on her hot center, she moved against his cock. She reached for the button on his jeans, but he stopped her. "No. First you."

He undid her jeans, and she lifted her hips to help him slide them off. She was wearing a matching lace thong. Heat raced through his veins. "God, you're so beautiful," he said as he ran his fingers along the top of her thong. She bit her lip and lifted her hips in response.

He went back to sucking her nipples as he moved his hand over her hip. Her breathing was getting faster. When he moved his fingers over her center, her breath caught. He moved down so his mouth was over her core, and her breath got faster still.

"Rhys," she moaned. He pulled the lace down over her hips. She helped him get it off and he dropped it on the floor. She watched him as he lowered his head to taste her.

She was wet and ready for him. And she tasted like honey, better than anything he could imagine. He licked her slowly with his tongue and then went in small circles. She fisted the couch cushions and made small panting sounds. He gently slid one finger inside her and then another, moving in a slow rhythm as he glanced up at her. She had her head thrown back and was biting her lip. The way she was responding to him made him even harder.

He put another finger inside her and sped up the rhythm, her hips matching his pace. He captured her with his tongue, and she fisted his hair, holding him against her. Her hips were bucking wildly, and she called out his name as she came. She looked incredible as she lay back on the sofa, and a wave of protectiveness washed over him. She was his. His red-haired, green-eyed Christmas angel, and he had no intention of being good. He was going to make sure they were both on the naughty list several times over.

CHAPTER 11

SCARLETT COULDN'T GET over the feel of Rhys's stomach. She'd never been with a man so cut. She ran her hands all over the taut ridges of muscle as he kissed and sucked on her neck and throat.

"Rhys," she moaned. "It's my turn to touch you." She smiled. "Take off your clothes."

"You like being in charge." He chuckled but did as he was told. He was something to behold when he was dressed, but naked? Naked, he was something else entirely. His body was chiseled as if carved out of stone. Not an ounce of fat anywhere, which might have been damned annoying if he wasn't so fucking hot.

She made him lie down on the sofa and then straddled him. His eyes turned a smoky gray, and he reached up and put his hands on her hips. She smiled as she started kissing his neck. She worked her way down his chest, touching and tasting every inch of him, and he groaned when she started sucking his nipples. She laughed and teased him some more. "What? You shouldn't dish it out if you can't take it."

He swore in response, and she moved further south until her mouth was over his cock. She let her tongue touch the very tip, and then she made small circles. First one way, then the other. Slowly, she drew more and more of him into her mouth, sucking and twisting her tongue.

Rhys growled her name, his rough voice sending tingles of pleasure through her. His hips started to move, and she matched the rhythm with her tongue.

"No, I want to come inside you."

Scarlett nodded. God, how she wanted that, too.

"Condom?" she asked, pulling away.

"There's one in my wallet," he said, his voice husky. She stood so he could reach it and watched as he tore it open and rolled it down over his cock.

Scarlett turned toward the arm of the sofa to grab a blanket for them, not that she was likely to need it when she had him to heat her up. Rhys stood and started kissing the back of her neck. She went to turn around, but he pulled her against him, cupping her breasts from behind. She moaned and arched into his hands.

He guided her to the sofa and pushed her gently onto her knees, kneeling behind her. "I want you like this."

Scarlett moaned. "Yes, God, yes." She was wet and ready for him; so turned on she couldn't think anymore.

Rhys rubbed her breast and tweaked her nipple with one hand as he moved the other down to her core. Her hips started moving in time with his fingers as he played with her center. He wedged his cock between her ass cheeks and rubbed it up and down, driving her wild.

"Rhys," she moaned, "*now*. I want you inside me now."

He bent her over and slowly entered her. It was so damn hot. She was vibrating with desire for him. He started moving slowly, but she pumped her hips faster. She needed more. "Faster. Harder."

Rhys complied, and within seconds, they both careened over the edge.

Scarlett leaned on the back of the sofa with Rhys on top of her. He was out of breath, just as she was. "Rhys."

"Sorry, I'll move. I'm too heavy." He started to shift his weight.

"No. It's not that."

"What then?"

"Do you have more condoms in your wallet? I definitely want a round two, if not three or four."

Rhys chuckled. "I knew you were going to be the death of me."

～

SCARLETT OPENED HER EYES SLOWLY, but the room was too bright so she closed them again quickly.

"Come on, sleepy head. Time to get up," Rhys called from the doorway.

She opened one eye. "What time is it?"

"Eight. It's bright and sunny out there. Time to start your day."

Scarlett groaned and rolled over. "You know what that means, don't you? It's effing freezing. Besides, it's way too early. I don't have to be at the spa until later this afternoon. Sunny texted me last night to tell me. I want to sleep in."

Rhys came over to the bed. "That's not what you said last night."

"That was then, and this is now. I seriously need more sleep."

"So you don't want the eggs and bacon I made for breakfast?" Rhys teased.

Scarlett brought the covers down again. "I wouldn't go that far. I *am* hungry." Food wasn't the only thing she was hungry for. Rhys had on those ass-hugging jeans and a blue sweater that made his gray eyes look bluer. Of course, now that she knew what he looked like naked, it wouldn't matter if he was wearing a potato sack. She'd still be hot for him.

"Not surprised," he drawled. "You worked hard last night."

Scarlett was sure her cheeks had burst into flames. She pulled the covers over her head as Rhys's laughter reached her ears.

He pulled the covers down again and leaned down and kissed her. "You're so cute when you're embarrassed."

She shook her head. "It's not funny."

"Yes, it is." Rhys chuckled again.

Scarlett's eyes narrowed. Two could play this game. She slipped out from underneath the covers and planted a scorching kiss on Rhys. She pressed her naked body against his clothed one and kept moving against him until she was sure he was rock hard, which took all of fifteen seconds, and then she sauntered into the bathroom. She turned and looked back over her shoulder. "Don't even think about coming in here with me." She closed and locked the door. *Take that.* She grinned at herself in the mirror and then took a quick shower.

Ten minutes later, she was dressed and at the table eating bacon. "This is so good."

Rhys smiled. "I'm glad you approve. So, what do you want to tackle first today?"

"You said they delivered the groceries, right?"

Rhys nodded toward a bunch of bags in the corner.

"Great, then we have a lot of cookies to make."

"Hudson and Sunny already dropped off your

baskets and the other decorations you asked for." Rhys pointed over by the Christmas tree.

"Excellent. After we finish the cookies, we can drop them off to everyone. I also have to go to the spa to finish up some last-minute touches and make the punch list. I know Sunny still has to deal with the fire inspector after Christmas. Something about checking the sprinklers. If all of my stuff is taken care of, she'll have less to worry about."

"Well, I'll clean up breakfast, and you get started. I'll help where I can, but I'm not much of a baker."

Scarlett leaned over and kissed him. "You can be my assistant."

"Does that mean you're going to order me around?" he asked with a twinkle in his eyes.

"Maybe. If you play your cards right." She winked at him and then scooted away before he could grab her. If they started something now, she'd never get the cookies baked.

Scarlett unpacked the groceries and got everything organized, including the baskets and decorations Sunny had picked up for her. She frowned. It was stupid. She should've been able to go to her apartment get them herself, but since the break-in, she just couldn't face it.

"Hey." Rhys came up behind her and put his arms around her. "It's okay, you know. You don't have to go back to your apartment until you're ready."

She shook her head. "What are you, a mind

reader? I know, but I should be ready. It should be okay."

"Honey, you suffered a major trauma less than a year ago. No one thinks any less of you for being freaked out by this. You do it when you're ready." He kissed her cheek, then pulled away and went to pour more coffee. "I do wish you'd let me hire a cleaning crew to clear it all up first."

He'd offered last night.

"I know, and it's sweet of you, but I'm afraid they'd throw something out that I want to keep."

"Let me know if you change your mind. Do you want more coffee?" Rhys asked, his hand hovering over a second mug.

"Please." She nodded. "I still think I'm going to look for a new place once the holidays are over. I don't want to live there anymore."

"You're welcome to stick around here if you want." Rhys placed the coffee next to her on the counter and went over to the sofa and sat down.

Scarlett's heart pounded in her chest. Was Rhys asking her to move in with him? Like, in a permanent way?

"I'll be leaving a few days after Christmas, but I'm sure Hudson won't mind if you stay here until you find a new place."

It was like being knocked on her butt again. Scarlett couldn't breathe. She grabbed the edge of the counter and closed her eyes, struggling to inflate her lungs.

Rhys was leaving. How could she have forgotten he was going? Or maybe some tiny part of her had thought last night would change things. It certainly had for her. She finally got her lungs to inflate.

When she opened her eyes, Rhys was staring at her. "Are you okay?"

"Yes," she croaked. "Coffee is hotter than I thought it would be."

"Oh." Rhys nodded. "Anyway, let me know if you want to stay here. I'll ask Hudson, but like I said, I'm sure he won't mind."

Scarlett smiled and busied herself unpacking the bags. "Sure. I'll let you know." Her voice came out much stronger than she was feeling, thankfully. She needed to get it together. No one had said anything about dating. This was just a fun fling as far as Rhys was concerned. He'd never promised her anything else, and she'd never asked. She could choose to be miserable about him leaving or happy about having a few more days with him. And it was Christmas Eve. There was no better time to choose happiness. She could practically hear her mom saying, *It's up to you to choose to be happy, my girl.*

Taking a deep breath, she organized the baskets and lined them with parchment paper. Then she put the red and green Christmas tea towels in each basket and flipped the edges over the sides so she could load the cookies inside and wrap them up. Then she wound the ribbon that Sunny had brought around the handle and finished it with a big bow tied on the top of the handle. For the first year, Scarlett was doing it without her mom, and it made her a little sad, but this time, she had Rhys. He made it tolerable for sure.

"All right, Rhys. Get your butt over here," she said as she moved the baskets so they lined the floor by the door. "It's time to bake cookies."

Several hours later, Scarlett loaded the last of the cookie baskets into the back of her SUV. All in all, it had been a very productive morning. Once she'd decided to just enjoy the moment and stop worrying about the future, things had gone smoothly. Rhys was much better at baking than he'd let on. She suspected he was good at all kinds of things. He'd certainly proved that last night. She made a mental note to get more condoms.

"What are you smiling about?" Rhys growled as he closed the tailgate. He bent down and adjusted his boot.

"Are you still grumpy about your cookies?"

"I'm not grumpy."

"I promise I'll make you more, but I refuse to give Miss Clara burned cookies—and it's *your* fault they were burnt." She mock-glared at him.

"You looked so cute in your apron with flour all over you," he said with a smirk. "I couldn't help myself. So, really, it's your fault." He wrapped his arm around the back of her as he kissed her and then dumped snow down her back.

"Ooow!" she yelled, but it was too late. Rhys had run to the driver's side of the SUV and was already in. She couldn't chase him anyway. She had her spike-heeled boots on.

She went around to the passenger side and climbed in. "Just remember, buster! Revenge is a dish best served cold. You can kiss those cookies good-bye."

Rhys grinned. "I'm sorry, but it was worth it. The look on your face was priceless."

"You just laugh it up. I promise you'll get yours." She gave him a wicked smile. "Okay, let's go. We have five stops to make, and it's already early afternoon."

"Where to first?"

Scarlett told him the list of people they had cookies for and told him to decide what order worked best for him. They started on their way. Scarlett sang along to the Christmas carols playing on the radio as they drove. They slowed up on Dead man's curve. There was a car accident. Lots of emergency vehicles. "I hope everyone is okay."

"Looks like that's the driver there, so I think it's all good." Rhys pointed to a teenager that looked pale and shaken, standing with one of the officers on the side of the road.

"Hey, did Striker ever call you back with more details?" Scarlett asked.

"No," Rhys said his knuckles whitened on the steering wheel.

"It's bothering you."

Rhys glanced at her and then looked back at the road. "I would have liked confirmation by now that Dr. Kyle was the intruder."

Scarlett glanced out the window. It had to be him. It made sense, and it sounded like he'd all but confessed. Besides, she *needed* it to be him. Rhys was leaving soon, and she couldn't face dealing with this without him. "Well, if it wasn't him, I think Sheriff Striker would have made a point of telling you. So"— she smiled at him—"we're all good."

CHAPTER 12

"I can't believe I'm eating a cheeseburger two nights in a row! I would never have done this in California!" Scarlett exclaimed.

Sunny laughed. "Right? It was all salads and smoothies. Sushi and vegan restaurants."

"Oh, my God, yes!"

Rhys looked across the booth at Hudson. "I don't think I'd like California."

Hudson started laughing. "No. Not if I had to eat vegan. I respect people who can do it, but I need a steak or a damned good burger now and then."

Rhys nodded. "Agreed."

June came by with the coffee pot. "Refill for anyone?"

Hudson nodded to his cup. "I'll take some."

"I can't drink any more coffee, or I won't sleep tonight," Scarlett said with a smile.

Rhys leaned over and whispered in her ear, "Who said you're getting any sleep tonight?"

She looked down at her now empty plate. Her cheeks were getting pink. He knew he should stop saying things that embarrassed her, but she was so cute when she blushed.

"No coffee for me, June," Sunny said, "but is there any of that apple spice cake left?"

He perked up as did Hudson.

"Apple spice cake sounds excellent," Hudson said.

June nodded. "Four pieces then?"

Sunny waited for Scarlett's nod before answering. "Sounds good. I've given up on sharing any food with Hudson. He always eats his share and starts in on mine."

June laughed. "Coming right up, ladies and gents." She started clearing the empty plates off the table.

"How come the diner is open on Christmas Eve?" Scarlett asked.

"Well," June said, "every year Jeb, the owner, says we should close but Nancy and I think we should leave it open. You just never know who needs a hot meal or some company. Christmas Eve can be lonely for some folks. We like to be here just in case."

"That's very sweet of you and I bet you get some people coming every year," Scarlett said.

"We do," June nodded in agreement and then took off with their dirty dishes.

"Scarlett, want to come back and see the kitchen?"

Sunny asked with a conspiratorial smile. "I'm thinking maybe you could help redo the space."

Hudson snorted. "You know you don't manage this place anymore."

She rolled her eyes at him. "Yes, I know, but I think Jeb needs to rethink a couple of things. Everyone loves the diner, so we want to keep the feel, but the furniture has seen better days." She pointed to the duct tape on the booth across from them. "Wi-Fi wouldn't be a bad thing to add and maybe some space for people to sit all day and work. Jeb has plenty of room to expand."

"Oh, let's go take a look," Scarlett said. Her eyes were shining. Now that the Wellness Retreat was almost finished, she needed a new project. She'd told Rhys as much. She had another couple of gigs going, but nothing big. He was glad she got along so well with Sunny, too. It was nice to think she'd have someone in her corner after he left. *If he left?* He balled his napkin up in his fist.

They got up to go, but Sunny turned back to give the guys a withering look. "Either one of you touches our cake, and you're dead meat." Rhys and Hudson held up their hands in surrender, and the girls made their way back to the kitchen.

"Have you heard from Striker?" Rhys asked.

"No. Have you?"

Rhys shook his head. "Makes me nervous. I've left him a couple of messages, but he hasn't responded."

"You think this guy Nathan Kyle isn't the intruder?"

Rhys shrugged. "I just want confirmation. I need to have this all tied up before I leave. I need to know Scarlett's safe."

Hudson leaned back in the booth. "So you're still going back to work for Black Thorn?"

"Yes. I...need to go."

"Why?" Hudson asked bluntly. "What are you going to find there that you can't get here?"

Wasn't that the question. But June showed up with their dessert, saving him—temporarily—from answering.

"Those girls told me to remind you not to eat their cake." June winked. "Don't worry. I took care of you." June set down huge pieces of cake in front of each of them, then arranged two smaller pieces in front of the girls' seats.

"June, you are the best." Hudson gave her a big smile, and she laughed as she walked away.

Rhys picked up his fork but didn't cut into the cake. "I guess I need to know for sure I can still do the job."

"Of course, you can. I would be dead if you couldn't do the job." Hudson ate a bite of cake.

"I got distracted, and I got shot. One of us could have been killed because of my mistake."

Hudson put down his fork. "Are you telling me you blame yourself for what happened? Are you fuckin' serious? A goddamn little kid ran into the middle of a firefight. Anyone in their right mind would hesitate rather than risk shooting a kid.

"The guy on the roof wasn't there before. If he had been, we'd have seen him. We didn't. So this wasn't on you. That whole clusterfuck happened because that stupid CEO client decided he wanted to be a hero and go see the site where his charity was helping to set up a school. Never mind it was a fucking hot zone. If he'd listened to us, it could've been avoided. You didn't lose your edge. You did your job exactly as you were supposed to."

Rhys let out a breath he hadn't realized he'd been holding. He and Hudson had never talked about that day. He always wondered if Hudson privately thought he'd messed up. That he wasn't as good as he used to be. He'd wondered if that was why Hudson was pushing him to stay home. "I guess I just want to be sure."

"Well, I'm sure. Hell, even Griffin told me you were on point, and he's a former Delta. It's damn hard to impress him. Why are you giving up every-thing you've got going on here to go back to Black Thorn?"

"Hudson, I don't have much going on here."

"Really? I'm thinking Scarlett wouldn't like it if she heard you say that."

"We're just...friends." He wasn't so sure he believed that, and he heard the lie in his own voice.

"Friends, my ass," Hudson said with a laugh, seeming genuinely amused. Then the humor faded from his face. "You've got a job waiting for you, doing the thing you love with a group of people who are excellent at what they do. You've got a woman you're crazy about, and you've got a place with one of the best views I've ever seen. What's missing? Why leave?"

"It's fuckin' cold here for damn near six months of the year! I hate the cold!"

Hudson burst out laughing. "Get long underwear. It's only cold here like that sometimes and usually when winter starts early it ends early. Sometimes Spring starts in February. Plus if it's cold, it just means you need to keep Scarlett good and close."

Rhys ate a mouthful of cake. It really was good. When Hudson put it like that, why *was* he leaving?

The girls sat back down and dug into their cake. Twenty minutes later, they were all on their way out the door. "I have to stop by the Wellness Retreat," Scarlett said, and everyone groaned. She laughed and held up her mittened hands. "I know, I know. But if I finish the punch list now, then I won't have to think about it again. I can just send it to Andy, and he'll take care of everything."

"Okay, but just in and out, right? It is Christmas Eve," Sunny reminded her.

"I know, and I promise." She crossed her heart.

"Thanks for having dinner with us. It was fun. Say 'Merry Christmas' to Clara for us."

Sunny smiled. "I will. And I'll give her the basket. She'll love the cookies."

"I'll love them, too." Hudson grinned.

Sunny swatted him. "You got your own cookies. You can't eat Gran's."

"Where's the Christmas spirit in that? Isn't it all about giving?"

Sunny shook her head but gave him a quick kiss. "You are incorrigible."

"Yup. That's why you love me." Hudson said as he helped Sunny into the truck and then closed the door after her. He went around and climbed in the other side and, a minute later, they were gone.

Rhys helped Scarlett into the SUV and then went around and got into the driver's seat. "So, we're going to the Wellness Retreat then?"

"Please," Scarlett said as she got settled in her seat.

Rhys swore. "My phone battery is low. I was preoccupied last night and forgot to charge it." He grinned at her and winked.

Scarlett pulled the cord out of the glovebox and handed it to him. Rhys plugged in his phone. On the way to the spa, Scarlett turned up the Christmas carols on the radio and made Rhys sing with her. Twenty minutes later, they pulled up in front of the entrance. Rhys reached over and grabbed the front of the Scarlett's coat. Pulling her close, he kissed her.

"What's that for?" she asked, breathless from the kiss.

"For being my Christmas angel." She looked so good with her eyes sparkling. Maybe Hudson was right. Perhaps everything he needed was right here. Rhys kissed her again. A long, slow, deep kiss that promised all the things he would do to her when they got home.

His phone rang, and he broke off the kiss. "It's Striker. I've got to take this."

"I'll go in and get this done. You talk to Striker. We'll be out of here in no time. I have plans for you later, and they may or may not involve eating icing off certain parts of your anatomy." She laughed and hopped out of the truck.

He lowered the window. "Scarlett, just wait a minute. This won't take long."

She waved at him but continued unlocking the door. Once inside, she went to the security panel and turned off the system. Rhys's nerves settled some when he saw the light turn green. Nothing had tripped the system or turned it off.

She blew him a kiss and disappeared inside.

∽

SCARLETT HUMMED to herself as she headed to the back of the medical wing. She'd made a list yesterday of most of the touch-ups needed. Only a couple of rooms were left for her to walk through. A smile stretched across her face as she walked into the first one and hit the lights. The room looked fabulous.

The soft gray walls with the light wood floors and the chrome chairs gave it a modern feel, but the use of the massage bed instead of an examination table made it feel more inviting. The fact that it was covered with a soft brown blanket and a crisp white pillow was just the additional touch that created a bedroom feel rather than an exam room. The cabinets were a lovely shade of brown that matched the blanket.

Scarlett walked around, examining every single wall and cabinet for any nicks or scratches. She bent over and checked out a floor tile by the end of the bed. There was nothing she could see, and if she couldn't see it, no one could. Satisfied, she straightened up and backed into someone. "Oh! You scared —" The words died on her lips. She put her hand on her chest and swallowed hard. "What are you doing here?"

~

"YOU'RE SURE?"

Striker's voice came down the phone line. "Yes, Kyle isn't the one who's been harassing Scarlett."

Rhys's mind went in five directions at once. "What about that woman who was with him when he came to the spa that time?" What was her name? She'd introduced herself at the Green Bean.

"You mean Megan Thompson? She's Kyle's some-times girlfriend, but no, she isn't involved either. We had a long talk with her. She said everyone knows about the stolen money, and since the body was found and the money wasn't with it, they all figured it was hidden at the spa. But it sounds like she didn't buy into Kyle's theory about the money still being around before news of the body broke. I'm sorry, Rhys. We don't have any other leads at the moment, but I'll keep you posted."

"Thanks." Rhys clicked off the call and practically bolted out of the truck and toward the entrance. He grabbed the door and pulled, but it wouldn't open. Scarlett hadn't locked the door after her, had she? He looked through the glass and saw the security system was glowing red. Someone had turned it back on remotely, which meant the doors were locked again.

Heart racing, Rhys ran back to the car, grabbed his phone, and dialed Scarlett. He could hear it ringing in the truck. *Shit, shit, shit.* He hung up. He could break in but the alarms would go off. The last thing he wanted was a bunch of deputies showing up with siren's blaring. As much as he admired Striker, he wasn't about to put Scarlett at risk that way. A silent approach would be best.

Rhys called Hudson, filling him in on the details, then ended the call and hurried back to the front door to wait. Heart hammering. Foot tapping. A few seconds later, it flashed to green.

Thank you, Sunny and Hudson. The door was unlocked, and backup was on the way.

Rhys opened the door quietly and slowly entered the building. Scarlett had only turned on a few lights. Good, he'd be able to find her without going through every room. He took a few deep, centering breaths as he crept down the hallway, letting his instincts take over.

$\sim$

"GIVE IT TO ME," Donna demanded, blocking the doorway. She had a large knife in one hand.

Scarlett shook her head. "Give you what?"

"Don't play dumb with me, bitch. I know you have it." She advanced a step into the room.

"The money, that's what you want, right? I swear I don't have it." She put her hands up as if to appease Donna, but Donna wasn't having it.

"Liar," she snarled. "You're the only one who could have it."

Scarlett shook her head. "No. There were dozens of workers in and out of here. If it was hidden in here somewhere, any one of them could have it."

"Do you think I'm an idiot? I checked." When Donna took another step into the room, Scarlett took a step back. She hit the end of the exam bed with her butt cheek. If she could get around the corner of the bed, she could put it between Donna and herself.

"You checked *all* of them?" Scarlett moved backward an inch at a time. She rested her hand on the bed. She was about four inches from being able to move behind the bed.

Donna nodded. "Most didn't have access to the whole area. Those who did, well, none of them are smart enough to hide the money. No. Only you and Sunny could have done that. I've searched Sunny's place when her grandmother was out, and it's not there. Plus, if Sunny found it, she'd have turned it over immediately. Everybody knows she's a straight arrow. You're the only unknown factor. So it's either hidden in the building, or you have it."

"I don't have it. I swear. I haven't seen it, and the whole building has been redone. If it were here, someone would have found it." Scarlett was very close to being able to step around the edge of the bed. She shifted all of her weight onto her back foot and tried to move right.

Donna must have realized what Scarlett was doing because she lunged at her. Scarlett's boot heel got caught on the leg of the bed, and she screamed as she went down hard on her behind.

Donna was there in an instant, leaning over her with the knife pressed to her throat. "Get up."

Scarlett was having trouble breathing, but she gave a slight nod. She tried to stand and realized there was a problem. "M-my heel broke." She held up the spike heel that had broken off the bottom of her right boot.

"I don't care," Donna snarled, waving the knife in Scarlett's face. "I said get up. Now!"

Scarlett rose slowly, using the bed for leverage. She stood on her left boot and balanced on the toe of her right. Her butt was killing her. She'd definitely broken something this time.

Donna came around behind her and put the knife to her back. "Now move."

Scarlett limped as best as she could out of the room. She looked both ways in the hallway, hoping to see Rhys. Surely, he knew by now she was in trouble. How long had she been in here? But the hallway was empty.

"Go to the right. We're going out the back door."

"Where are you taking me?"

"Funny, I was going to ask *you* that. We're going to wherever you have the money hidden."

Scarlett half-turned toward Donna. "I told you, I don't have the money. If it's hidden somewhere in the spa, I don't know anything about it."

Donna shoved the knife blade up under Scarlett's chin, so the very tip of it broke her skin. Blood trickled down Scarlett's neck. "If you don't want me to keep cutting, then you better tell me everything. I'm about done playing around."

Donna's eyes were flat and mean. She meant

every word she said. Scarlett closed her eyes. Fear paralyzed her body. Was this the terror her mother had felt before she died? Scarlett let a sob escape her lips. She prayed her mother hadn't known what was coming because the terror she felt right now was all-consuming.

Scarlett opened her eyes. "I don't h-have the money. I don't know what happened to it." Donna pushed the knife blade up a little harder. More blood oozed down Scarlett's neck. "B-but I do have money. I can give you money." Scarlett was determined she was not going to die like this. She was going to do everything possible to live. No matter what it took.

Donna eased up on the knife a bit. "How much? How much can you give me?"

Scarlett saw a flash of movement. Was she imagining things? She focused on the corner of the hallway behind Donna. She was sure she'd seen Rhys's face there a second ago, although it might have been wishful thinking.

"How much?" Donna demanded.

"A m-m-million dollars," Scarlett mumbled. She needed to make a plan. Donna had a knife. What could she use against her? Her fingers closed around the spike heel in her hand.

Donna's eye's narrowed. "You have a million dollars? I don't believe you."

"I-I do." She swallowed her fear and spoke more clearly. "My mother was a famous chef. She had her own cooking show. She left the money to me when she died." Scarlett shifted the heel in her hand so she had a better grip on it.

Donna put a bit more pressure on the knife as she studied Scarlett's face. "Fine. You can transfer it to my account. We'll do it somewhere else. Now turn around and walk."

Scarlett saw a flash of Rhys again. This time he was close to the ground. He crawled out from behind the corner, moving slowly. Slinking like a panther. Donna grabbed Scarlett's hair and was in the process of turning her around when Scarlett plunged the heel into the woman's neck. Rhys came up from behind, hitting Donna on the back of the head and grabbing the knife from her hand.

Donna dropped to the floor with the green spike heel sticking out of her throat. Her eyes rolled back in her head.

Moments later, the hallway filled up with cops and security men. They'd just arrived as Scarlett was making her escape.

Rhys grabbed Scarlett and crushed her in a bear hug. "Oh, my God. You scared the hell out of me! Are you okay?"

Scarlett could only nod. She wasn't able to breathe, but she didn't want to let go of Rhys. She couldn't. And he must have felt the same way because he scooped her up and carried her out of there. He set her down on one of the buttery soft leather chairs in the lobby, then sat across from her on the coffee table. "Are you really all right?"

"Yes. I'm okay. I think I broke my ass again, but other than that, I'm fine."

Rhys grinned. "I think you're good then."

The EMTs went by with a stretcher, and Scarlett had a horrible thought. "Did I kill her?" she whispered. Just the idea of it made her queasy.

"No." Sheriff Striker appeared by the edge of her chair. "You got her in the soft tissue of her neck. There's some damage but she's going to live."

"Oh, thank God." Scarlett's shoulders sagged. Another EMT came over and moved Rhys out of the way. The man cleaned and covered the small cut under Scarlett's chin and left her with some instructions on caring for it.

"You up to answering some questions?" Striker asked as the EMT left.

"Can't it wait 'til tomorrow?" Rhys growled as he sat back down on the coffee table directly across from Scarlett's chair. Just then Hudson walked in.

"Scarlett, are you okay?"

"I'm fine."

Rhys grunted.

Scarlett put her hand on his arm. "Really I am and it's okay. I'd rather talk and get it over with now. Tomorrow is Christmas." She nodded at Striker. "Go ahead and ask." Just then, the EMTs brought Donna by on a stretcher. They nodded at Striker but kept going.

Striker sat down in a chair next to her. "Why don't you tell me what happened?"

He took notes while Scarlett explained the situation in detail. Rhys kept his fingers locked with hers.

"And what about you?" Sheriff Striker asked Rhys. "Anything to add?"

Rhys explained what he'd done. Striker took more notes. "It looks like you got lucky," he said to Scarlett. "This could've gone very differently if Rhys hadn't been here."

"No. Scarlett saved herself. I was just there to pick up the pieces," Rhys said.

Scarlett smiled.

Rhys squeezed her hand and then turned back to Striker. "So do you think Donna killed Windemere?"

"It seems likely. Megan Thompson said she thought Donna was having a fling with Windemere, and we know Donna is flat broke. She got in over her head with some real estate deal that went bad, and now she's in desperate need of cash."

"Huh. Any ideas on the money? Hudson asked. "I'd prefer if it were found so no one else gets any bright ideas about going after Sunny or Scarlett." Hudson shot her a quick smile.

Striker shook his head. "It's still a mystery. I spoke with Stone MacLeod from the FBI earlier. They're still searching, but it's not looking good. The money has been gone for a while now, and they have no real leads."

Scarlett tuned out the men as she glanced around the lobby. It had turned out well. The desk was made of a dark wood that matched the leather chairs, which she could attest were quite comfortable. The floor was a lighter wood with beige and gray throw rugs placed in a few highly trafficked areas. The waterfall fountain behind the reception desk would add ambiance to the space once it was turned on. All in all, it had worked out well. When she spotted her green coat, which she'd laid across the desk on her way in, everything clicked into place.

"Well, that's it for now. Feel free to take her home," Striker said.

Scarlett glanced up at Striker. "I think I know where the money is."

"What?" Striker and Rhys both stared at her in disbelief.

"The money. I think I know where it is."

"Where?" Rhys asked.

Scarlett pointed. "Can you hand me my coat?"

Rhys frowned but called out to a passing deputy, who grabbed the coat and handed it to Scarlett.

"Thanks." She pulled Montana Moose out of her pocket. She'd noticed some stitches in his back when Andy had first handed him to her. "This is the only thing left of the original spa that hasn't been gone through or completely replaced." She extended her hand, and Rhys gave her his pocketknife. She cut the stitches, then reached her hand inside the moose's back. A second later, she pulled out a USB stick and handed it to Striker.

"Bitcoin. This is the key to open the bitcoin account."

Rhys cocked his head. "What makes you think he put the money in bitcoin?"

"Well, if the FBI can't track it, and he didn't have it with him when he died, there are only a few possibilities. You can't hide that kind of paper money easily, but you can conceal bitcoin no problem." She brushed the hair out of her eyes.

Rhys cocked an eyebrow. "Should I ask how you know about bitcoin?"

Scarlett smiled. "No."

Striker grinned. "I'll check it out and let you know, but I think you're on to something here. Thanks."

Rhys stood and offered Striker his hand. The two men shook. Rhys signaled Hudson he was leaving, and Hudson came over and gave Scarlett a hug. "I'm so glad you're all right."

"Thanks. Me, too." She stood, balancing on one foot.

"Sunny wanted to come, but I wouldn't let her. She sends her love."

"Tell her I appreciate it, and we'll catch up after Christmas."

Hudson nodded. He clapped Rhys on the back and then went over to talk to Griffin and the other Brotherhood guys.

Rhys smiled down at her. "Ready?"

"Yes." A wave of fatigue hit her hard, and she wobbled a bit. Rhys scooped her into his arms, took her out of the lobby, and tucked her into the SUV. If she weren't so damn tired, she might be embarrassed, but on the other hand, maybe not. She was getting used to having Rhys take care of her.

Too bad he's leaving. She'd forgotten for a moment, something that seemed to keep happening. She closed her eyes. She would have to work on distancing herself from him, or her heart would be broken when he left. Who was she kidding? It was already too late for that. At least she still had a few days left with him.

The ride home seemed to take no time at all. She blinked. She must have fallen asleep. Now that the adrenaline had left her system, her butt and back hurt. Everything was getting stiff, and it seemed like a monumental effort just to get out of the SUV.

"I've got you." Rhys picked her up and carried her directly into the bedroom. He helped her undress and get into a warm flannel nightgown. He tucked her into bed, and a few minutes later, he joined her. But he didn't try to seduce her—he just kept her curled up against him as she fell asleep.

CHAPTER 13

SCARLETT OPENED an eye and looked around the room. Rhys wasn't there. She listened but couldn't hear him moving about in the cabin. She sat up slowly and groaned. Everything hurt. A quick glance at the clock told her it was nine, which was later than she'd slept in a long time. Images of the night before flickered through her mind, and she shivered. But it was over. For good this time.

She managed to haul herself out of bed and head to the bathroom. No sign of Rhys in the main room of the cabin. Her heart raced in her chest. Had he left without saying good-bye? She looked around wildly for a note, but there wasn't one.

Deep breaths, Scarlett. After the first flush of panic faded, she realized Rhys wouldn't leave like that, with no warning, especially after the attack last night. He wasn't that type of guy. He would make sure she was okay first.

She took an aspirin and then took a long, hot shower. Feeling more human, she toweled herself dry, dried her hair, and got dressed in her Christmas outfit—a long red velvet skirt and a cashmere forest green sweater. She took one last glance in the mirror. She looked damned good for someone who'd been held hostage the night before. Or at least she thought so.

She opened the door to the main room and found Rhys on the sofa, drinking coffee. "You're back," she said.

He stood and turned around. He froze in place. "You look...beautiful."

She smiled. "Thank you. You don't look so bad yourself." He had on dark jeans and a dark gray sweater that made his eyes look the color of steel. "So, what's for breakfast?"

Rhys grinned. "Food before presents. You're my kinda girl."

"Wait, what? Presents? But I didn't get you anything." She frowned. How had she forgotten to get Rhys something for Christmas?

"You're going to make me some cookies. That's good enough."

She nodded but promised herself she would get him something nice before he left—something to remember her by. "So, what did you get me? Oooh, a big box. What's in it?" she said as she walked across the room. She came around the edge of the sofa. He patted the cushion next to the box. "You sit here."

She lowered next to the box, and he sat down across from her. Her belly rolled. He seemed too serious. Her heart picked up in tempo. "Rhys? What is it? What's going on?"

Rhys looked at her but didn't speak immediately. She suddenly noticed he'd turned on Christmas music. It was playing softly in the background, and he'd turned on the twinkle lights on the tree and front porch. It was darker outside, and snow was beginning to fall. It was a beautiful sight, one she would love under normal circumstances, but this wasn't normal. Rhys was freaking her out.

"Rhys?"

"I've been doing a lot of thinking." He paused. "Things are different than I thought they were, or at least, I feel differently about them."

"You're not making any sense."

Rhys took a deep breath and started again. "When I got shot, I thought it was my fault and I'd lost my focus, my edge. I thought it might be time for me to stop doing what I love. I had doubts for the first time ever.

"But then I started protecting you, and I realized I still had my edge. But part of me wouldn't fully believe it until I went back to the Middle East. I figured I couldn't be sure unless I faced up to everything. But last night, watching that woman hold you at knifepoint, Scarlett, I could focus. I could function. I knew what I had to do to save you. I don't need to prove anything to anyone, least of all myself." He took her hands in his. "Scarlett, if it's okay with you, I'd like to stay here in Canyon Springs…in this cabin with you."

Scarlett blinked. "You're staying?"

He nodded once. "If you're okay with it."

Tears welled up in her eyes, and her throat closed over. She had wanted him to stay so badly, but it hadn't seemed possible. "That's the best Christmas present I've ever had." She smiled at him and then leaned forward and kissed him.

"There's just one thing," Rhys said.

"What?"

"You've got to help me with the cold! I can't stand it."

Scarlett burst out laughing. "I know what you mean. It's so much worse than I thought it would be. I guess we'll just have to keep each other warm." She was leaning over to kiss him again when the box next to her made a sound. Scarlett froze and frowned at Rhys, one eyebrow cocked. "Did that box just whimper?"

Rhys grinned. "Why don't you open it and find out?"

Scarlett narrowed her eyes at Rhys but reached

for the flaps. She opened them and looked in the box. A pair of big brown eyes looked up at her. She gasped as she reached in and picked up the cutest puppy she'd ever seen. "Oh, my God, he's adorable! It's a he?"

Rhys nodded. "It's a he. I know how much you love Huck, and I figured you might want some company. I'll have to travel some for work."

She cuddled the little puppy to her chest, and he licked her chin. "Wait. You have a job already?"

"Yes. That's where I was this morning. Hank Patterson offered me a job with the Brotherhood Protectors. I was signing paperwork and getting everything in order. They function even on Christmas. Oh, and I had to pick up this little guy."

Scarlett couldn't control it any longer. Tears streamed down her face. "This little guy is exactly what I needed for Christmas." She smiled at him. "You always seem to know just what I need." The puppy nibbled on her ear, and she laughed.

"That's my job as your boyfriend," he said, his steely gaze turning warm. "To know what you need and take care of you. This little guy will help out when I'm not around."

"Rhys, I thought after my mom died it would take me years to feel happy again. To feel loved and cherished. To feel like I belong. You've done all of that for me and more. I can't tell you have much it means to me. How much you mean to me. I'm so glad you're staying here with me."

"Scarlett, you're my Christmas angel. I never want to be without you ever again." Rhys leaned forward and captured her lips in a scorching kiss.

ALSO BY LORI MATTHEWS

Callahan Security Series

Break and Enter

Smash and Grab

Hit and Run

Brotherhood Protectors

Justified Misfortune

BROTHERHOOD PROTECTORS

ORIGINAL SERIES BY ELLE JAMES

ABOUT ELLE JAMES

ELLE JAMES also writing as MYLA JACKSON is a *New York Times* and *USA Today* Bestselling author of books including cowboys, intrigues and paranormal adventures that keep her readers on the edges of their seats. With over eighty works in a variety of sub-genres and lengths she has published with Harlequin, Samhain, Ellora's Cave, Kensington, Cleis Press, and Avon. When she's not at her computer, she's traveling, snow skiing, boating, or riding her ATV, dreaming up new stories. Learn more about Elle James at www.ellejames.com

Website | Facebook | Twitter | GoodReads | Newsletter | BookBub | Amazon

Follow Elle!
www.ellejames.com
ellejames@ellejames.com

 facebook.com/ellejamesauthor
twitter.com/ElleJamesAuthor

Made in the USA
Monee, IL
22 December 2020

55272072R10105